RECLUSIVE

SKULLS RENEGADE MC BOOK 9

ELIZABETH KNOX

CONTENTS

Cover design by Charli Childs, Cosmic Letterz Cover Design

Editing by: Tania Jabbour Varela, Knox Publishing

Formatting by: E.C. Land, Knox Publishing

Proofreading by Jackie Ziegler, Knox Publishing

Photography by: Reggie Deanching, R plus M Photography

Cover Model: Darrin James Dedmon

❀ Created with Vellum

ACKNOWLEDGMENTS

MY AUTHOR TRIBE: IRIS, GG, JEN, AUDEN, MICHELLE, ERIN, LINNY, JP, BRYNN, JA, & CHRISTINE – I know we may not speak every day, but know I love and adore y'all more than I can write down in words.

MY BETA'S, LAURA, TANIA, CHAS, MICHAELA, KEANNA, RACH & COURT – Have I told y'all that I adore each and every one of you? I do! Thank you for continuing to give me the best feedback an author could ask for.

My Editor, Tania – You push me, girl. With every book we work on you push me harder, encourage me when I need it, and tell me when I'm downright crazy. I can't do any of this without you, and your friendship means the world to me.

MY BLOGGERS: JENNA, JEN, SHANNON, CHASIDY, ANGIE, HEATHER, LIZZIE, JAMIE, AMANDA, DEANNA, ANGELA, REBECCA, ALICIA, JAMIE, CHRISTIANA, CHRISTIANN, KRISTIN, VALERIE, ANNA, CIA, LEANNE, LINDA,

EMILIE, SHASTA, NICHOLE, ERIKA, STARR, GWEN, NICOLE, ASHLEY, KEANNA, MYN, HEATHER, PRIMROSE, JADE, DUSTY, JEN, KRISTEN, LENA, CAROLINE, JES, TRACY, ANN, MEAGHAN, TINA , CHARLEI, NIA, MARIAN, BECKY, VANESSA, PHILOMENA, JAMIE-LYNNE, ASHLEY, LINDA, KATHLEEN, ASHLEY, DANIELLE, LAURA, KEANNA, TAI, KATHY, & SHIRLEY – Goodness gracious, y'all are about to eat Trick up for dinner and want him for dessert too. Don't say I didn't warn ya!

KBB, MY BABES! – You all have been so patient as I've been taunting you with this story for months. I truly hope that it's well worth the wait and that y'all enjoy it as much as I do.

DEDICATED TO THE BROKEN ONES,
You may feel like you're damaged beyond repair, as if you're not worth loving, but you are.
Remember, even broken pieces can be put back together, and so can we.
Just keep breathing.

PLAYLIST

Insecure — Svrcina

I'm so tired... — Lauv ft. Troye Sivan

Last Hurrah — Bebe Rexha

Sober — Demi Lovato

Tie Me Down — Gryffin, Elliy Duhe,

Common — Zayn

CHAPTER ONE

The course of true love never did run smooth
~ William Shakespeare

Trick

I'm standin' here in this fuckin' CVS knock off of a pharmacy in the card aisle. Why am I here? Well, if I could answer that I think today things would be a lot clearer. Today is Valentine's Day. You know, the day when you spoiled that one lucky bitch who gets to suck your cock dry every night. Considerin' I have one of those now, I thought it would be a good idea to pick her up a card and some chocolates. I figured what the hell, I'll be in and outta here in less than five minutes. It was gonna be simple, I'd head straight for the candy dressed up in heart packaging, grab a whole bunch of different varieties of chocolate and grab a cute card on my way out.

I've been standin' in this aisle for at least ten minutes, looking at the different messages on these cards. There's some for boyfriends, husbands, girlfriends and wives. Shit, even some for kids. I've looked through almost every one of these and nothing feels good enough to buy for Angel, my girl, my fuckin' ol' lady. We haven't known each other for very long, but I didn't have to. The moment I laid my eyes on her I knew that she needed me. I don't believe in love at first sight or any of that shit, but it sure as hell was something.

I pick up this orange card and think to myself, *orange... for Valentines? Really?* But figure what the hell. I open this fucker up and what it says would hit me deep in my heart if I had one.

'We may have just met,

But I'm ready for the rest of our lives.

Just don't give up, no, not yet.'

Corny as shit, but fuck it'll do. Angel and I aren't in love or any of that shit, but I find myself caring so much about the girl, even if all she's done thus far is driving me insane. Having her in my life has been worth the insanity and all the headaches she gives me. I wouldn't trade it for the world. It's funny, I'm buying chocolates and a card for a girl that I've only known a few weeks when I didn't even do this shit for serious girlfriends back in the day. Just as I'm walking up to the register, I see a cute teddy bear and grab it, then walk up to the register to pay. I hand the dude a fifty dollar bill and head out to my bike, putting everything safely away in my saddle bag before riding back to the club.

The drive is a short one and not interesting to say in the least. I'll take boring though. After being in the slammer for all those years, it's sure nice to have some peace and quiet for a change. While I've seen a bit of interesting shit over the last few weeks, it hasn't been as hectic as jail. It's ironic how we're animals confined in a cage, yet it's one of the most terrifying places of your life, never knowing who has your back or who wants to put a knife in it. Out here... Well, I know exactly who's on my side.

I get back to the club and see a few of the bikes are gone. I'm sure they've just gone to handle some business, but I check my phone just to make sure everything is going smoothly. I pull it from the back of my jeans and don't see any missed messages. Everything's all clear from the looks of it. I park my bike, dismount and grab Angel's presents from my saddle bag before heading inside. I see Daisy on the couch with Ryder playing in front of her. Looking around, I don't see another person in sight. "Everyone throw a party and didn't tell us?" I ask her, chuckling.

"Oh, nah. Three's company is in the back, making an amateur porn video from the sounds of it. A few of the guys are helping Kyle put some finishing touches on his and Meech's house since the contractors went AWOL and the others are doing who knows what." Over the last couple of weeks everyone in the club has started calling

Pain, Chaos and Maria three's company because they hardly ever leave each other's sight. Not that I can blame them for it. If my girl had gone through what Maria went through, I'd be doing the exact same thing and stickin' close to her ass.

"Yeah. I'm sure they want to get everything settled before Michelle gets too big in her pregnancy where she's uncomfortable. Plus, they have three times the shit to buy for those girls." I reply. Kyle was fucked up a few months back in an accident. We honestly didn't know if he was going to pull through. It was touch and go for so long, but thank fuck he did. His girl has triplets on the way and all of his girls need him in their lives. "Angel in the back?" I ask Daisy, already knowing the answer. Of course, she's in the back. She hardly ever leaves our room.

Daisy gives me a slight nod just as her little boy starts blabbering on, in his toddler language.

I walk down the hallway and turn the corner to where Angel and my room resides. With the way the club is set up, we have one of three rooms on this side with no other neighbors. It gives us privacy, but it's not like I need it. I'm not getting laid and even if I was, I like it when others can hear my girl screaming her throat out. I think everyone just wants to keep away from us, knowing how mouthy and sassy Angel can be.

She may look like an Angel, but she sure as hell doesn't act like one.

"Hey Angel," I greet her as soon as I walk in the door

and shut it behind me. She's sitting on the bed flipping through some sort of girlie magazine.

Her eyebrows cock up as soon as she sees a bag in my hand. "What do you have there? Heroin?" I know she's joking, but even though she has dry as fuck humor, it hits me hard, deep in my stomach whenever she jokes about using drugs. It's the last thing I ever want her to do again. My only priority is about keeping her sober and healthy. And happy, I want her to be really happy.

"Well, it's Valentine's Day and I wanted to show you that you're special to me." I say, digging my hand into the bag as I walk over to her, I pull out the card and chocolates. She tosses the card on the ground and within what feels like five seconds she has that poor little teddy bear's head ripped right off.

She holds the teddy bear's body in one hand, while his head is in the other. "*This* is how special you are to me."

"Jesus…" I grumble, glaring at her. I just need to get used to this shit. It's never going to change. Fuck this. I wrap my hand around her dainty little throat and stare into those light eyes of hers. I don't fuckin' speak because I don't have to. I'm showing her who's in charge and she needs to get it through her damned thick skull.

She tries to speak, but no words come out. I smirk at my grip around her throat before meeting my eyes back with hers. "Are you trying to say something?'"

Angel nods slowly.

"I'll let you talk after I say my peace. Listen up, and listen good. You're my ol'lady Angel, whether you like it or not. It's the way it is and the way it will always be. I'm gonna spoil you, however much I want. I'm gonna show you that even though you treat me like a piece of shit, I will never do the same to you because you're worth more than that. You might not have ever wanted me baby, but you're fuckin' stuck with me. Learn to live with it. You know as well as I do that things could've been so much worse for you." I release her neck and press my lips right against her temple before heading to our door, opening it and slam it behind me as I walk away from her.

The woman frustrates the living hell out of me, but I mean every word, and so much more. She just doesn't understand that I'm going to cherish her through everything, no matter what she fires at me. I'm going to care for her just the same.

CHAPTER TWO

"Someday we will find what we are looking for. Or maybe not.
Maybe we'll find something much greater than that."
~ *Anonymous*

Angel

With each passing day I'm here I feel more like a
stranger. These aren't my people, and they aren't my
family. It doesn't even feel like Pain and Chaos are my
family most of the time. I'm more of a nuisance to them
versus a sister anyways. It's the day after Valentine's and
the queen bee, Elena, decided there should be some sort
of festive party thrown in honor of the holiday. So, here I
am making sure the icing on my skank cake is up to par. I
run the knife over the side of the cake, ensuring the ratio
is equal on both sides and can't help but wonder why I
even care.

Oddly enough, I want to fit in here, even if I never will.

It's not like I'm some girl who grew up in this life or fell for the big bad biker. No, my story is so much different. I'm the charity case that the old, somehow still good looking biker decided to dedicate his time to. Trick isn't my boyfriend but, he sure as hell acts like he is. He calls me his girl, his ol'lady and I still don't quite understand what it means. Is it like being married? Does it mean more than marriage? From what I've seen I think it does. I see Daisy and Seamus, Elena and Reed, and even my brothers with the girl they share. An ol'lady is something that I'm not used to, and I don't know if I will ever be.

I pick up the plate that my skank cake is on and bring it out to the main area of the club, walking it over to the pool table that we've thrown a blanket over. It's essentially a buffet table now, riddled with desserts, and an abundance of meat options. "What's that you have there?" I hear his voice before I see him, noticing the curiosity lacing his tone.

Setting the plate down, I turn to look at Trick and think about what I'm going to say. I was nothing but a cunt to him yesterday and I do want to make up for that. I just had a bad day and we're all entitled to them. Funny enough, Trick has never held one against me. He may stomp off all pissed like, but he always comes back. With the way I treat him I sometimes wonder why he comes back. It's not like I kiss him or let him fuck me. "It's called skank cake," I start off telling him, watching his eyebrows furrow before he lets out a belly laugh.

"Skank cake?"

"Yeah. It's a vanilla cake with marshmallows, M&M's and other delicious delights stuffed into one sugar filled orgasm."

"A sugar filled orgasm, is that so?" His cyan blue eyes light up. "I have a feeling that's not the cake we're talking about, Angel." For the first time since I've *been* with Trick, if that's even what I can call it, I think he's flirting with me.

"Well, you're just going to have to try a piece and let me know how you like it." I say to him, hoping deep down that he does enjoy it. I love to bake sweets when I have the opportunity. I'm no Betty Crocker but I can get the job done.

Trick looks past me, and I turn to see Reed signaling him over for some reason. "Gotta go, babe. I'll be back in a bit. Behave, will you?"

"I always behave." I firmly state, flashing him a devilish smile.

"If that isn't a crock of shit, I don't know what is." Trick mutters under his breath as he walks away, and for some reason I want to reach my hand out and grab him. I don't want him to leave. Every day I fight something inside of me, telling me that I don't need him to help save me, that he's only with me because I am a charity case. But then there's this other side of me that believes I may be able to have something feasible with him, something real.

Something that I've never had with anyone before.

Never have I been an actual person to any man, I've always been an object.

I look around the room to the abundance of people. Some I recognize where others I don't and spot my brother, Chaos, sitting by himself on one of the couches. We don't really get along at all but he's a friendly face in a crowd. Well, sometimes friendly. He won't admit it, but I believe he still resents me for not staying clean. Both he and Pain were able to get off the drugs and create a better life for themselves, where I just remind them both of someone, we all hate – our mother.

She chose the drugs over us too many times to count, and here I've been doing the same. I'm not a mother, though, so it's different. Right?

"I'm shocked you didn't lock yourself in your room with a needle in your arm." He grumbles out, crossing his arms.

"Jesus. Isn't the point of me being here to stay clean? It's kind of hard not to think about being high when you keep bringing up drugs." I snap. The thing that pisses me off the most about Chaos is that he knows how hard it is to stay clean. He has felt every single thing I have, and so has Pain. In all honesty, he knows better.

I don't want to hear whatever retort comes out of his mouth, so I rise from my seat on the couch and go over to the newly dubbed buffet table, scanning it for something awful and sinfully delicious. I grab some sort of pink cake pop and toss it in my mouth, chewing just as I hear her. "Fuck. Why is she still here?" I see the girl named Jenna roll her eyes at me from across the table and don't understand what sort of problem she has with me.

I think about staying silent, but biting my tongue has never been my specialty. "I could say the same thing to you. You're here all the time and don't live here. Can't you just do us all a favor and leave?" If someone wants to be a bitch to me, I have no problem being one back. Especially when I've done nothing to deserve being treated in such a way.

"You're real cute, sweetie. What gives you the right to think you can talk to me like that when you've already done so much shit?"

"Is that some sort of joke? What have I ever done to you?" I ask, furrowing my brows, confused beyond belief. Actually, I'm not confused. I'm pissed. "If I ever did anything to you I'd remember it. I never forget someone I've crossed." I snap at her cockily.

She reaches her hand back and smacks me flat across the face. The bottom of her wrist hits my nose and all I feel is a loud pop with a jolt of pain. I pull my hand to cover my face, not sure what just happened.

"What the fuck is wrong with you?!" I hear Chaos roar, charging in our direction. I think he's sticking up for me once, being the big brother I've always needed him to be. But when he grabs me by the wrist and shakes me, I know I'm wrong. "Do I need to repeat myself? What the fuck, Angel?! What did you do?!"

I stand here staring at him, unable to say anything. Why is he assuming that I started this?

"What the fuck is wrong with you?!" He screams in my face, so loud that the entire room goes silent. Everyone is staring at us, all of the attention focusing on our fight.

I glance around, seeing the judgmental looks that others are shooting my way. There's no possible way they're doing it to my brother. No, he's one of them. It's all me. "Everything! I fucking wish you'd left me to die in that place. I wish I wasn't even brought here in the first place. It's not like you want me here to begin with!" I cry out, shoving Chaos quickly out of my way as I run out the front door.

I don't know what I need most right now: air, or freedom.

CHAPTER THREE

To make a difference in someone's life you don't have to be brilliant. Rich. Beautiful. Or perfect. You just have to care.
~ Mandy Hale

Trick

Reed and I are in his office having a chat when all a sudden, I hear Angel raising her voice, and not in that good type of way. She sounds upset as all hell. He and I share a concerned look and I dart through the doorway, down the hall to see what the hell just happened. I'm met with seeing Angel's small frame flying right out the front doors to the club and both Jenna and Chaos sharing a mutual look.

I approach them, anger already starting to boil in my body. "Anyone want to tell me what the hell just happened?"

Jenna rolls her eyes, "I might've gotten into a skiff with the clubwhore. I don't get why all of a sudden we need them, we've never needed them before and all she's going to do is stir up trouble with the couples."

Chaos laughs like this is the funniest thing he's heard in ages and it takes everything within me not to ball up my fist and plummet it into his mouth.

"Clubwhore? Angel is my fuckin' ol'lady!" I hiss out at her.

"Oh? Well that's unexpected. Angel's always been a whore. How do we know she's not just going to start fucking what doesn't belong to her?" I'm amazed at the set of brass balls Jenna thinks she has, but I'm no idiot. There's something more going on here.

"You two knew each other before she was clean, didn't you?" I ask, already knowing the answer.

She shrugs, "We may have crossed the same paths a time or two. It wasn't a pleasant experience for me."

"Anything else happen?" I'm not talking to Jenna, it's fuckin' pointless to talk to her. This time my focus is right on Angel's brother, Chaos.

"She basically said she wish she was dead."

"Really?" I growl at him.

"She'd be doing us all a favor." Jenna says under her breath. Does she think I can't hear her? I'm over this shit.

I scoff at her. She's going to understand how I feel about this situation here and now. "Listen to me here and now. I don't give a fuck if you knew her when she wasn't at her best. You don't stir up any shit with her, and you sure as fuck don't disrespect my girl. If you do, you'll pay for it."

With raised eyebrows, her expression grows cocky. "Good luck with that. I think Reed would have something to say about it." It's like she thinks she's untouchable. But boy, does she have that wrong.

"Nah. Don't think Reed would appreciate his sister being nothing but a fuckin' cunt to a woman who deserves as much respect as you do. He'll think it's pretty fucked up." I don't stick around to hear anymore words that spill from her mouth. Instead I head out the door that Angel went through.

As soon as my hands push the door open, I see her sitting on the railing of the makeshift deck. She's holding the column, or... well, she's leaning against it.

"Angel," I say coolly, approaching her slowly. I know that I only got part of the story about what just happened. Chaos didn't say jack shit, and I'm not really one to trust what Jenna's said. Honestly, I don't give a fuck if she knew her before. That doesn't give Jenna the excuse to treat her like shit.

She snaps her head around to me, tears flooding in a heavy stream over her cheeks. "What?!" I see her nose is bruising and now I'm wondering what the hell happened in there.

"Did she fuckin' hit you?" I ask, quickly approaching her. I skim my hands over her face and look over her features. Angel squirms the entire time, my analyzing her obviously making her upset. I just

15

want to make sure she's alright. Even if we both know that she isn't.

"I don't belong here, Trick." She completely goes into left field. "I don't feel like I do, but it's obvious. I'm not one of you and I never will be. I belong…"

"Shit, Angel. You don't belong anywhere besides with me. And before you even say it, you don't belong in the ground." I skim my fingers along her cheek, careful to make sure it won't hurt her one bit. "You might be a feisty bitch, but you have no clue just how special you are. Do you?"

Her eyes go wide, shock crossing over her face. "No part of me is special,"

"That's where you're wrong. *Every* part of you is special, even those ugly parts inside of you that you don't want to admit are there. You have 'em babe. I have 'em. We all do."

She remains completely silent, simply staring up at me.

I sigh before telling her what I know she needs to hear. "This. *Us*. It's not for show. We're a couple, Angel, whether you fully want to believe it or not. I think you know by now that I'm not the type of man who is going to say sweet shit just to say it. I say what I mean, and mean what I say. I know that being thrown into this life is something that you never wanted, that you never looked for yourself, but it's where you are. But it's important that you're not in this alone. I'm with you every step of the way. For every good day and every bad one. I made a commitment to you, girl. One I don't think you fully understand yet. Shit, I made a promise and I'm not sure if you know it, but I don't ever break a promise."

Angel doesn't make a peep. My heart is beating heavy in my chest as I lay all this shit out on the line for her. Never in my life have I said anything like that to a woman before, not even ones I had been with for years. I'm in a new phase of life, though. I wrap my arms around her small frame and bring my lips to the back of her head. "I'm never going to let anything happen to you." It's something I know that no one has ever said to her. She's never had the best people in her life from what I know, but shit does she need to hear it.

She turns her body around on the railing and brings her hands over my chest, until she's cupping my face. I'm not sure what she's doing, never seeing her become this quiet, this sincere in her movements. Before I know it, she's standing up on the railing, bringing her lips against mine. Her touch is slow and loving, those soft silky lips of hers getting to know mine for the very first time. I take my hands and hold her firmly, showing her that I don't want her to stop. I want us to both keep exploring one another in the way that we are right now.

I allow her to take the lead, knowing how quickly her mood always seems to shift. Sometimes, I don't think she really knows what she wants. So instead of taking the lead I'll let her do that, this one time.

She slips her tongue into my mouth and mine meets hers in a sweep of passion. I almost feel like a young man, like the very first time you kiss a woman. I'm sure as hell not a spring chicken anymore, but shit does this woman make me think that I am.

The sound of the door opening is enough to startle her, making her rip her lips from mine. Her eyes are fearful as she stares at the doorway. What she's afraid of, I have no idea. I don't give a damn about who's coming through that door. I just stare at Angel and all of her beauty, "That was nice. We should do it again sometime."

She giggles, laughing like I've never seen her before. So free in this moment, her guard completely down. "I'll make you work for it."

"Oh baby, I have no doubt that you will."

CHAPTER FOUR

I'm starved for connection, not attention
~ Anonymous

Angel

I run my hand along my face at the sound of Trick's alarm clock playing that ridiculous song. He still doesn't tell me what the name of it is, insisting that one day I'll finally get it. What he doesn't realize is that it won't click for me. I barely listen to any music as it is.

Rolling over, he lies on his back mouth open, snoring away. I jab him in the arm and wait, hoping that it'll wake him right up. It doesn't, but this man could sleep through a zombie apocalypse. I can't understand why he thinks a low alarm on his phone is going to wake him up. Unlike him, I can wake from a dead sleep at the slightest shift in noise.

"Trick!" I hiss loudly, smacking him. He doesn't even flinch. Bastard!

Finally, I roll over to the other side of the bed and toss my legs over the side. I get up on my feet and walk around the other side and throw the damn phone half way across the room, watching as it hits the wall. It shatters into a few big chunks as the sweet sound of silence greets me. I knew breaking it would do the trick! No pun intended.

A grumble greets me, "Was that really necessary?"

I throw my hand on my hip and turn around to look at the old fool. "Really? Your ears must be going 'cause how in the hell can't you hear that atrocity going off?!"

"It wasn't even loud. Did you turn my volume down?" He asks, cocking an eyebrow.

Shit.

I knew his alarm would go off this morning, just like it does at seven am every day, so after he slipped into dreamland, I turned the volume down on his phone. "I knew you fuckin' did it. If it was where it was supposed to be, my ass woulda' been up."

"Bleh-Blah," I grumble. He's probably right, but there's no way in hell I'll admit that to him. He's got a big enough ego as it is.

He slides out of bed clad in his jeans and t-shirt. Last night being the very first time he slept in the bed with me. Trick has slept on the futon in the corner of our room until now. There's a giant hole in the middle with the stuffing coming out, bumpy in random places and he tells me it's fine. Somehow, I highly doubt that it's fine. I know a few places to sleep where the concrete would be more comfortable than that. "Last night was… nice." He says it like a girl would, making me want to laugh, but I don't.

Looking over to him, I nod. "Yeah, it was." We didn't fuck or anything close to it. We kissed and cuddled like two teenagers with a crush and honestly, it had to be one of the most intimate experiences of my life. I've never had anything like that with any man, never have I felt so…precious. I could never find a word for it at first, of how Trick would make me feel.

In the very beginning he aggravated me. All he wanted to do was sit around and watch me, ask me questions, get to know me. But of course, I was going through withdrawal. I either wanted to throw up, or murder someone. Sometimes it was both, at the same exact time.

"I'm gonna go outside for a smoke." Trick tells me as he walks out the bedroom door. I get up and put a bra on, knowing it's pointless to try to go back and get any more shut eye because it won't happen. Once I'm up, I'm up.

I walk out of our bedroom and go into the kitchen, stomach growling and all. For once, I'm alone. Normally there's two to three people scavenging for food, needing to throw something in their stomachs. I open the cupboard that has the cinnamon cereal I like, grabbing the box and dig my hand in there, taking a handful and toss it in my mouth. I don't need the milk, or the bowl. I'll caveman eat this shit up any day of the week.

As I'm chomping the delicious sugariness in my mouth, I can't help but think back to the previous day, and what Chaos did. He and I have always had a complicated relationship, ever since we were little kids... but what did I ever do to him where he wouldn't try to comfort me after I said that the world would probably be better off without me? Pain would've never let me think that, but then again, Pain is the sensitive one. Chaos is just an all-out dick, there's no wonder Maria needs them both. Pain is too emotional by himself, and Chaos is too much of a raging asshole, but together they must make the *perfect* man. Ugh, I'll never understand their relationship, but I don't have to. As long as they're happy, that's all that matters.

Yesterday's flow of events circulates in my mind. Jenna's expressions. Chaos' tones. Trick coming outside to comfort me. If I know anything about being here, it's that almost everyone doesn't want me to be here. I feel so much like an outsider because I am one, and that won't change. I begin to open drawers that I never have before and find some rope amongst a whole bunch of duct tape, pens and note pads. Ah, this must be the junk drawer. I stare down at the rope thinking about what I said yesterday, thinking how easy it would be to just tie myself up and end it all.

"Sticking your filthy hands in my cereal, hmm?" Trick

says out of nowhere. I jump at least a foot in the air before turning back to look at him.

"This isn't just your cereal. Everyone can eat it. It's not like you have your name on it." I hiss out, shoving another handful into my mouth as I slyly shut the drawer.

He snickers, "You'd better turn the box around, Angel."

I do as he asks, coughing as I see his name written awfully on the box. "You were saying?"

"Oh, shut it. It's your job to feed me."

"Mhm," He mutters, walking over in my direction, he yanks the drawer open and looks inside of it. "What's so interesting in here?"

I shrug my shoulders, "Nothing,"

"You're a shitty liar. I saw you staring at the drawer for a good five minutes before I said jack shit to you. What was it? Were you staring at the rope thinkin' how you could hang yourself?" His smart-ass remark is accurate and I can tell that he knows he hit the mark. "Jesus, Angel."

"I don't feel like I'm wanted here. I'm barely holding it together, and when stuff like... what happened yesterday pops up it just doesn't make me feel good. It makes me want to..."

"What die? Or get high?"

I can't help but feel judged for having the feelings that I do. "Both, I guess. Sort of."

"Damn Angel stop worrying about shit. None of that

is on you anymore. You know who the one person who has to worry is? Me. It's my job to worry about you and handle shit. The only thing you need to be concerned about is livin'. Let me worry about the rest."

He makes it sound like it's such an easy thing for me to do, but it's not.

It's probably the hardest thing he could ever ask of me.

CHAPTER FIVE

*Sometimes painful things can teach us lessons that we think we
didn't need to know*
~ GoodLifeQuotes.com

Trick

I've been sitting in church for the last ten minutes,
waiting for the stragglers to arrive. We're only waiting
on Reed and Seamus at this point. Even Dmitri showed
up on time, and he drives in from a further distance. I'm
not really sure how he mended things with Reed, but
they did. Slasher is even forgiven for his actions, but he
doesn't come around too much. Only when absolutely
necessary. Rumor has it that he's working a lot with his
girlfriend, Katya, on her side of the business. Who
knows, that type of work could suit him better. If it does,
great. I only wish him the best.

The door bolts open and in comes Seamus and Reed, both gracing us with stern expressions. I take a closer look at Seamus and see his right arm is riddled with blood. I can bet you I know what he was doing. "Glad you're all here. As you all know we've been keeping Rafael under lock and key for the upcoming auction. It's going to come up quite quickly, so I need to make you all aware of what your roles are, but before we get into that there's a few other logistics." Reed gains all of our attention. I can't speak for the others, but I listen closely. Rafael Ramirez is the former leader of the Mexican Cartel, if not the slimiest human on the planet. There was discussion on what to do with him when he was removed from the throne, if that's what you want to call it, and it was decided that Rafael would be sold into damnation like many of the women he subjected the same fate too.

"With the help of Mariana Petran, we've secured the location to be an abandoned hotel on the outskirts of Nashville. It's right off of a main interstate and provides plenty of parking for the amount of people we believe will show up. We are going to be assisting Mariana and Ion's people in assuring that nothing happens that shouldn't, adding to the amount of muscle. If anyone so much as makes you feel uneasy, or like they're there to stir up trouble, you know what to do. Trick, Dmitri and Chaos will be working inside the auction." Reed looks to the three of us. "You three will be the closest to Rafael, ensuring that no one tries to off him before he's sold."

Chaos stands up from his seat and slams his fist down on the table. "You want *me* to protect him, after everything he did to Maria? It's not happening, Prez. Over my dead fuckin' body."

Reed is a good Prez, but like all of us – he's human. "I think Chaos might not be the best choice to keep an eye out over Rafael," I add, trying to show Chaos I understand his views. If the same had happened to Angel, I'd rip Rafael's fuckin' throat out and not think twice about it. "It's a sensitive issue and you can't blame him for feelin' the way that he does," I tell Reed.

I see him thinkin' about saying something smart, but he shouldn't. The smartest thing he can do right now is replace Chaos with someone else and not say anything that will cause emotions to run even higher.

Reed follows Chaos' lead and stands up, eyes trained on our brother. "You want Rafael to pay for everything he did to your girl, don't you?"

Chaos doesn't dare reply. Honestly, that was a stupid as fuck question to ask him. Of course, he wants Rafael to pay.

"The only way for him to suffer in the horrid ways you want him to, is to make sure he doesn't get popped. You want him to regret every decision he's ever made? Make sure he stays alive. Make sure that he's around long enough to feel it all." Reed's words are obviously resonating with Chaos. I know that when they were trying to figure out what to do with him, there was a lot of backlash for not killing him. In the grand scheme of things, this shows everyone that the Ramirez family no longer has any say of what happens in Mexico – that they're irrelevant. Instead, the Lopezes run Mexico now and with the change in leadership I think there will be even greater changes coming.

"I want him to suffer."

"Then make sure that he does," Reed tells him, "Go out to the shed and make sure he suffers a little more today. Pretty sure the pain is starting to fade from Seamus' session with him," Reed looks over to Seamus who keeps his expression flat. "What do you think?"

"There's not enough pain that he can feel. Go have a few rounds on him, Chaos. It might make you feel better rememberin' that he's our bitch until the auction happens."

"Yeah." He murmurs. I can't blame him for being pissed that Rafael is even here. "Don't take me off his detail. I'll make sure he doesn't die until he's supposed to." What Chaos is asking of Reed is shocking... if I was in our Prez's position, I don't know if I'd do what he wants.

Reed nods, "I know you won't let me down. But before we end our session, the Lopezes are coming to town. Francisco's son, Dante will be accompanying him. . We need to solidify our alliance with them, make it official in a sense. Before we were simply under 'the enemy of our enemy is our friend' tactic."

"Whatever we can do to help, we will." I speak up. The

dawn of a new age is coming, and with it so much change will follow.

I'm ready for the impending changes, and I'm more than prepared for our club to officially become allies to the Lopez family. It's about damned time if you ask me.

CHAPTER SIX

*"Soon, when all is well, you're going to look back on this period
of your life and be so glad that you never gave up."*
~ *Anonymous*

Angel

Trick got out of some meeting called 'church' that I still
don't really understand, and insisted we go get some
grub. The club owns this bar named Bubba's a few miles
away. I've heard of it before, but I've never been in the
joint. Not until just now as Trick and I walk through the
front door.

From the outside it looks like some mountain hillbilly
bar, but on the inside it's something completely different.
"Trick, you want firecracker chicken!?" I see a short,
gorgeous girl shout from the other end of the bar. She
has a cloth, wiping it against a glass.

"Sure thing, brat. Get my girl here a Tennessee burger with loaded fries, and I want one of those peanut butter brownie sundaes you girls have been whippin' up too."

The girl smiles brightly yelling "Okay. Grab a seat. I will be back!" before she walks back into the kitchen.

I want to know who she is, why she seems to know Trick so well and why the fuck he calls her brat. He hasn't even given me a fucking pet name and I'm his girl-friend, or ol'lady or whatever you call it. Jesus, I never thought I'd get aggravated about something like this. Especially because I didn't even want to be with him at first. I wanted *nothing* to do with his old, damaged ass. But over time, I've seen the way he is... how his heart is as big as this entire planet, how he cares more than anyone I've ever known, and more importantly, how he treats me. Trick sees my flaws and accepts them. He's the one person that I know will never give up on me, no matter how much I fail or try to push him away. He'll just push me back, and I've accepted that.

"C'mon, let's grab a seat." He says, grabbing ahold of my hand, he leads me towards the back of the restaurant, and we take a seat in an intimate booth.

I can't seem to shake what plagued my mind just a few minutes ago, and after sitting in the silence, I ask. "Why did you pick me, and not one of those Russian dolls?"

Trick raises his eyebrows in surprise, before coughing into his hand and sitting up a little straighter. Oh boy, this is gonna be *good*. I can already tell. "I didn't want a Russian doll. The moment I saw you, I knew that I needed you. And fuck me for sayin' this, but you sure as hell needed me to. We didn't have insta-love or any of that shit, Angel. But the moment I saw you I knew that we had somethin'."

Sometimes I really feel like I'm in some romantic comedy about a man and a woman who are damaged beyond repair but end up finding happiness in one another's arms. We end up sitting here for a bit chatting about pointless bullshit and our food comes out, and for the first time, I think we're on a date. "Can I ask you something else?" I ask him, tossing two fries in my mouth after I've smothered them in ranch.

"You're gonna ask either way. You always do this you know, ask me if you can ask a question but yet you've already asked one, so you might as well ask if you can ask two." He winks at the end, causing me to roll my eyes at him. Trick's always a smartass, even when he doesn't have to be.

"Why haven't you given me a pet name?"

He cocks his head back and laughs, taking a sip of the soda that the girl brought out a few minutes ago. "Damn, baby. You don't get it, do you?"

"How could I get it? You haven't given me one!" I grumble, crossing my arms. I'm the only one who doesn't have a pet name. Maria is *Taquita*, Elena is *Siren*, Michelle is *Princess* and I know for a fact Daisy has one too. I just can't think of it!

"Why do you need a new one when you already have

one, Angel?" He wiggles his eyebrows in front of me, causing me to scoff.

"You can't use my name as my pet name!" I argue, which just causes him to chuckle in response. Whatever. I'm not going to win this fight.

He laughs, before sliding out of the booth. I wonder what it is that he's doing, but I see him grab a few napkins, and just as he bends down, I see his shirt shift a bit. It reveals a tattoo that I haven't seen, but he's never taken his shirt off in front of me before.

"When'd you get that?" I ask, pointing to his back.

He seems surprised that I've asked, maybe it's because the two of us don't know a lot about one another's pasts. "About five years back, I got it when I was on the inside. It had been a few years since I'd been under the needle and I just needed somethin' new."

Wait. He said the slammer. "You were in prison? What for?" How didn't I know this?

Trick shrugs, obviously not wanting to talk about it. I don't give a shit, though. I want to talk about it and one way or another he'll tell me what happened. "Why were you in prison?"

He sighs, running his hand back through his hair. "I should've known better than to tell you. Of course, you'd badger me for info. To sum it up, I took the fall for someone who we couldn't sacrifice. It was better that I spent a few years locked up versus him. I'm replaceable, and he isn't."

"What? That doesn't make any sense," I say, grabbing my own drink, I take a sip of the grape soda.

"Prison never makes sense, but you wouldn't understand that."

I scoff, "Actually, I do. I've made my way through a couple of times, all related to drugs of course. One time I got mixed up with the nasty crowd, they paid me in heroin and told me if I sold for them that I'd get my shit for free, so of course little old me did just that. The police found me trying to work a deal and I was processed. It was my first major offense, so the judge took sympathy on me… I was lucky, I guess."

"You're not the type of woman I thought you were," He murmurs lowly. I'm not really sure where he's getting at. "But I'm not the type of man you think I am."

For the first time since I've met Trick, I feel like we're really beginning to learn who the other is.

CHAPTER SEVEN

*We are not haunted by the dead. We are haunted by the living
and the graveyard of memories they leave in our heads.*
~ Nikita Gill

Trick

*Rain is pouring from the sky, heavier than it has in ages. For
some reason I have an eerie feeling wash over my entire body,
like something isn't right. I'm not one of those people who get
the heebie-jeebies, but today I sure as hell feel like I am.*

*Everything over the past two days has gone insanely
wrong. Nothing, and I mean nothing could have prepared us
for this. We had a plan and it blew up in our fuckin' faces. You
can't be responsible for the actions of other people, though.
Nothing you ever plan for can guarantee you'll be successful in
the end when third parties are involved. In this case, we're the
ones that are fucked.*

Reed pulled the trigger and by God, I hope I wiped that gun clean to where they'll only find my prints. Jesus. We were so sloppy. Mistakes happen in the heat of the moment. If I've learned anything in life, it's just that.

I know that there was no way we'd get back there in time to get the gun before the cops did, and I was right. There's only one thing to do, and that's to prepare my family for the future, I'll most likely end up living.

I've just made it to my sister's house, she and my nephews are the only remaining family I have left. Everyone else is dead or chose to stay away from the two of us. Their loss, though. We're pretty rad people, even if they think we're just low life outlaws.

I get to Janine's house and place my hand on the storm door, hearing the creak the years have caused as I open it. Her front door hasn't shut in years and the tough bitch won't let a man do anything for her. It has to be her way or the highway. She's got balls bigger than any man I know, and considering she's my little sis, I let her get away with this shit.

"Anyone home?" I holler, walking into the kitchen. I saw her car parked out front, so I know she is. The boys are probably upstairs playing that new video game. What's it called, Halo? They told me they get to kill aliens. Shit, I should know. Their father isn't around, so I'm the next best thing. I spend a lot of my time over here when I'm not at the club, being around for them as much as I can. Janine may argue with me most of the time when I want to change a light bulb or fix a leaking sink, but I'll still end up getting the job done. It's not that she isn't appreciative of the help, *she just doesn't want to rely on a man – even if I am her brother.*

"Janine? Cody? Josh?" I shout, wondering where in the hell they are. If they'd gone out into town, they surely would've taken the car.

I make my way through the entire house, going upstairs to check both of their rooms and then come back downstairs to check the living room and Janine's room. Pulling out my cell, I call her up and she doesn't answer, but I hear her phone. I decide to go to where I hear it ringing, and head in the direction of the basement. Before I even get to the stairs, I see that there's blood on the railing. My heart beats heavy in my chest as I make my way closer, knowing that this eerie feeling from this morning wasn't just a feeling – it was a warning.

I put my phone in my pocket and pull out my Glock, training it in front of me. Slowly, I walk down the steps one at a time, being as cautious as I can. Janine would never leave her phone somewhere, so I know something's up. She gives the boys enough shit about it.

I'm on the last step and that's when I see her, blonde hair sprawled out in a pool of crimson. I set my piece on the ground and rush over to her, flipping her body over to see her face and I already know. There's no bringing her back. She's alabaster, her skin clammy and cold. Yet still I press my head to her chest to see, just hoping that somehow my baby sister is still alive. We've lost so many people, there's no way that I'm losing her too!

The reality of what's happened hits me, coming through my body in full force. I'm angry, yet at the same time I want to empty the contents of my stomach all over this room. I set her body back down against the concrete and grab my Glock, pulling out my cell phone I rush up the stairs and call Reed. He answers within a few rings, "Janine is dead, and I can't find the boys. I need help, Reed. Someone did this shit!" It's all I say before I hang up and continue to search the property.

Janine's house backs up to the woods, so I have a fuck ton of land to search. I can only hope that they're still alive, that they somehow got away. I glance around the landscape and see nothing out of the ordinary, everything seems to be as it always is – but it isn't.

I go from a steady walk into a quick run, needing answers as soon as possible. Cody and Josh have a treehouse deep in the woods, one that I built them when their dad left. They were just little kids who needed an escape from the shit they had gone through, and I wanted to give them somewhere they could go. Every boy needed that, especially these two.

I come up on the treehouse and place my hand on the wooden ladder, pulling myself up one rung at a time. As soon as I stick my head up, I see red Nikes, Cody's shoe of choice and just like his mother, he's gone. The weight of the world comes crashing in around me, not understanding who would do such a thing. I want to give up, but I can't. Josh is still out there.

Somewhere – he's out here somewhere!

I jump down from the treehouse and see my brothers coming from the distance. Reed is leading the group with Seamus and Kyle behind him. "What the fuck happened?" Kyle asks, and god, wouldn't I kill to know.

38

I hear a shout from the distance and all our heads snap in that direction. "Who would that be?"

"The new prospect, Enzo. I brought him out to help."

"Thank you," I nod, darting out in the direction of him. In a little over a minute I'm where he is, seeing him standing over a third body.

Jesus Christ.

Approaching Josh, I fall to my knees and pull him into my arms. For the first time in years, tears come rolling over my face in an uncontrollable way. I've had many losses over the years, but this has to be the greatest loss I've ever faced.

My entire world has come crumbling down around me.

"We will find out who did this," Reed promises, I look over to him with anger rushing through my veins.

"We'll find who did this and make them pay." I correct him, speaking in a tone that I would normally never dare to.

I jolt awake from my nightmare of memories that haunt me almost every night. It's been years and yet I can still smell the blood that coated their bodies. I can see their faces, looking as if they were filled with peace when we all know that it was anything than that. They would've been terrified out of their minds.

I sit up from my position on the couch, wiping my hand across my face, pulling myself out from that hell and remember the one thing that still haunts me. I was on the inside for five years and it was the anniversary of their deaths. I received an anonymous note, telling me that there was an eye for an eye, plus two more for good measure. I knew what it meant, and I knew that the person who killed my family sent it. There was no mistaking it, not in the least.

In moments like this, I feel a touch of regret for taking the fall for Reed, wishing that I was the one who never wiped off that gun, because if I didn't – they might still be alive.

There's no use thinking that way, though. The past happened and there's not a damn thing that anyone can do about it now. There's only one thing I can do – find the bastard who did this and make them pay. Reed promised me vengeance, but he's still failed to follow through. I know how important it is for me to be here for the club, and now for my girl, but I will find whoever did this, and I will make sure that they pay for every action they made.

CHAPTER EIGHT

Sobriety is never owned. It's rented, and rent is due every day
~ PaintedPlum.com

Angel

Trick shot out the door early this morning after falling asleep on the couch last night. He seemed different than usual. I can't really put my finger on it, but he was a bit jumpy. "I'm glad I caught you. We need to talk," Elena, the Prez's wife, starts to tell me.

"We do?" I reply, wondering where this sudden need to talk is coming from. We've chatted on occasion when the boys have been around, but never one on one.

Elena waddles her way in front of me and puts her hands on both hips. "Yep, I think it's about time we had this chat. I've been givin' you way too much slack around here and shit hasn't been getting done. You need to start pullin' your weight. The rest of us ol' ladies all do."

I'm confused. She's never brought up the fact I need to do chores or whatever the hell she's suggesting before. "What do you mean?"

"I mean, you need to start working. Daisy bartends when she can. Jenna still helps with the Russian dolls when she's around, Maria helps out at the bar, and Meech cleans the club. You need to start contributing round here too. I'm gonna pop in a few weeks which means I'll be out of order and can't help out. So, what're you gonna do around the club? We have a few options…" Elena goes on to list a plethora of jobs that she says we could use help on, and as she continues, the previous sounds worse than the last. I really don't want to be cleaning toilets around the club. I understand Meech has been around for a while… but how good of a job can she be doing if she doesn't clean the porcelain thrones? I don't blame her, though. I don't wanna clean whatever comes out of these guys asses either.

"The fridge is almost always empty," I shoot out, "There's hardly ever food in there and whenever I'm hungry I just end up eating cereal. What're the guys eating?"

Elena doesn't make a peep. She's not answering me cause' she doesn't know. Yep, I'll take cooking over cleaning up shit stains!

"I'll cook and put it all in the fridge. That way all the guys have to do is heat it up and grub out. Sound good?"

Elena smiles proudly as she replies, "That sounds great! I can't wait to see what you come up with."

"Don't you worry about that. Let me get to cookin," I tell her, and watch as she runs out of the kitchen. I go over to the massive fridge/freezer combo that we have and tear open the freezer door, seeing all sorts of frozen meats. Opening the fridge, my eyes land on various sauces and a decent mix of veggies.

Of course, these jerks won't eat it as is. I roll my eyes and take out some salmon from the freezer, walking over to the microwave, I place the meat on a plate and set the defrost setting. I'm gonna make these boys a teriyaki salmon stir fry they won't ever forget.

I feel like only ten minutes or so has past when I'm putting the servings into Tupperware and placing them in the fridge for the guys. I just need to get to the grocery store and get some more supplies to make more food. I doubt this will last til' the end of the day. I figure I'll just use the credit card Trick gave me. He won't mind. I'm sure of it.

I'm about ready to leave the kitchen when Elena comes back in. "You're done already?" She asks, and I nod.

"Yep, it's all in the fridge."

Elena pulls open the door and grabs one of the containers, taking off the lid and sets it on the counter. Before I know it, she has a fork in her hand and I can't do anything but stare at her as she picks the container back up and digs the utensil in the stir fry. Grabbing a heavy portion, she slides it into her mouth. The next thing I know, she's dropped what I worked so hard to create and is running towards the sink.

"Jesus! That's disgusting!" My heart sinks into my stomach and yet again, I feel like I can't do anything right around here – because I can't. It's been proven time and time again. All I keep doing is somehow fucking shit up and letting everyone down.

No matter what, I'm always going to keep doing that. There will be no way out of it. I wonder if failing people is in my blood. If my parents passed it down to me like a damn disease. It wouldn't shock me, in fact, it'd probably explain quite a bit.

There's only one place I know where I need to be – and it sure as hell isn't here.

———

My steps are slower than usual as I enter this place. I wonder if my body remembers the things that I've gone through in this house, on that particular bed. The way I felt so free and relaxed, the poison that takes every bit of agony away from me. After this day, I know I had to come here. I know that I need some sort of release, or else I'll end up caving under all of the pressure. I don't want to die. I just need help. I need something to make my life just a tiny bit easier, if only for a day.

There's a part of me that didn't want to come here, probably the piece of me that thinks about what Trick will have to say about all of this, but he doesn't understand. He's never been an addict. He's never felt the release that the drugs give you, how your every worry in the world obliterates before your eyes. The only worry that rests upon your shoulders is the continuation of life – to still breathe.

I don't want to be like I was before. I want to be so much different, a better person than I've ever been. Coming here is haunting and honestly, it's quite terrifying too. I take a seat and sit down on the dirty mattress where I've spent most of my days and put the tiny pill in my mouth.

I just need some good old fashioned sleep, and I'll be sure to get it now. Sleeping better than I have in weeks.

CHAPTER NINE

I never needed drugs. Everything I loved destroyed me enough
~ Word Porn

Trick

After a long day of prepping for the upcoming auction, I'm ready to fill my stomach and faceplant into bed next to Angel. I park my bike in front of the clubhouse doors and dismount, walking inside to my girl.

"Hey Trick. Long day?" Maria asks, and I nod.

"You have no idea. Can't keep doin' shit like this," I chuckle in response. I look around the club and see a few of the regulars, even spotting Wrath and a few of his buddies. He's Michelle's dad who never really stuck around much before, but maybe since she's growing her family, he feels the need to stay. Not sure, don't really care to be honest. "Angel around?" I ask her, hoping she'll just point me in the direction of wherever it is that Angel has run off to.

Maria shrugs her shoulders, "Not really sure. I haven't seen her all day. Elena did though, ELENA!"

Elena pops her head out of the kitchen at Maria's call. "What's up?"

"When's the last time you saw Angel?" Maria questions her.

"Sometime this morning. She made some sort of stir fry thing for the guys to grub on and my pregnancy did *not* agree with it at all. Ugh, I hate being pregnant. There's so much food I know I'd love to eat, but my body just doesn't agree with my choices at all. Fucking sucks!"

I listen to what Elena says and her babbling words as she continues. Opening my phone, I tap on the tracking app that Lucian, a friend of the club, had designed for us a while back. It allows us to put a hidden application on our girls' phones, running in the background to where they don't even know it's there. The best fuckin' security you can ask for! All I have to do is open this app up, and I can see wherever it is Angel's phone is on a map. It's showing me that she's in her room, so I'm not worried in the slightest.

"Oh no, I hope I didn't offend her. Shit! I spit out the food right after I took a bite. All of it was just too much for me and the baby, the aroma, the taste. But damn does that girl know how to cook. I think we should keep her on cooking duty for a while."

I smirk at the fact I'm being shown Angel really has

nothing to worry about. She's fitting in just fine, even if she doesn't see it. Sure, there are a few hiccups along the way, but when aren't there? When you mix personalities, there's bound to be some sort of eruption.

After a few minutes of miniscule chit chatter, I make my way into the kitchen and open the fridge. Flat in front of me there are a couple containers of what Angel must've cooked earlier today. I grab one, take a plate out from the cupboard and pour some of the food onto the plate, before nuking it in the microwave. I want this shit sizzling hot while I scarf it down.

Reed gave us each a few tasks to complete throughout the day, some of it being pretty heavy, construction work at the hotel where the auction is being held. It's coming up in just three days and there's a shit ton to do still. It needs to look as good as it can with all these people flying in from around the globe.

Tomorrow I'll be heading back out there to get a few more things finished before going over security with Reed. I've developed somewhat of a blueprint where our joint forces with Mariana and Ion Petran, and our Skulls brothers will be stationed during the auction. If anyone tries to do anything shady, they'll hate that they even tried. Shit, it'll be much worse than hate. They'll feel their mistakes for eons.

The microwave beeps, signaling me that my food is ready and I open the door, pulling the plate free and walk back to our room. Inserting the fork into the stir fry, I pop a good serving into my mouth and moan. Elena sure wasn't kiddin'. This shit is full of flavor, but she did get one thing wrong. It's delicious!

Upon opening the door, I have to do a double take. Angel's phone says she's here, but the room is dark and she sure as hell isn't here. "Angel?" I call out her name, just in case she's asleep on the futon or somethin', but I know better.

Fuck, I think to myself.

"Maria!" I holler, walking back out to the main area of the club.

She shoots out from behind the bar, "What's up, Trickster?" She giggles at the last bit, laughing at my new 'name' as she calls it. She's cute and short, so I let her get away with it. Plus, she's Latina, which means she's batshit crazy. So maybe that's why I let her get away with it.

"Where are your guys, they seen Angel lately?"

A scoff greets me and there's no mistaking who it's coming from. "She's probably high, knowing her habits."

"Wait... where's your truck?" Maria asks me as she heads straight over to the front window. Peering through the curtains, she looks back at me. "It's not here."

"Like I said, she's probably shooting it up somewhere. Did you leave any cash lyin' around, Trick?" Everything about his tone is accusatory, like even if she is high, and that's a big if, it's automatically my fault. There's no reason to assume she's high at all.

"You wanna shut the fuck up and help me find your sister?" I'm trying to think of all the places that I know Angel would be before I end up making a mistake and plummeting my fist through her brother's jaw. I know they have a rocky relationship, but it's like he'll never forgive her for being an addict. I know it's hard to forgive someone who's hurt you, but after a while, you can't hold onto that pain anymore. Someday he's gonna have to let it go, and by God, I hope it's soon.

Chaos doesn't bother to reply to me, showing me that I'm on my own. Not shocked there, though. I grab a set of keys from the grocery getters that we have on a table in a fishbowl and walk out the front door, unlocking whichever car I managed to grab. I smile at the luck of the draw, a Jeep Wrangler. This will most certainly do.

After I'm inside the SUV, I tear out of the driveway and head for the first place I could think she is. It's the last place we picked her up, and the most likely possibility. A small, old, worn-down house in a shady side of town. I want to hope she isn't here, but the moment I see my truck, I know she is. At that, I pull out my cell and send a group text to the brothers, telling them that I need someone to grab my truck from this address. There's no way I'll be able to drive two vehicles, especially when I don't know what kind of shape Angel is in.

Hopping out of the Jeep into the cold February air, I head straight to the door of the house. Not bothering to knock, cause who the hell would in a place like this. I search the entire joint, going room to room, seeing the peeled back newspaper on the windows. Watching water drip from leaks in the ceiling. Cobwebs coat most of the place, with what wallpaper was probably quite popular back in the day falling off the walls. That's when I spot her body, curled up on a mattress.

Her arms are drawn to her, sleeping like she's in the fetal position and I pray harder than I ever have before that she's still with me. The sad truth is that Chaos is probably right, and she could be high right now but I'm hopin' that she isn't.

I'm hopin' that she's doin' better for not only herself, but everyone who loves her.

I grab her by the shoulders and flip her body towards me, looking on her arms and even her feet to see if she has any track lines. Her arms are good, but she still has her shoes on, so I check anyway. I doubt that if she shot up she'd had enough time to put her shoes back on, but it's better to be safe than sorry.

She's good, thank god. I sigh in relief, running my hand along her forehead, wondering what the hell is goin' on with her. Why would she want to come back here?

There's only one way I'm gonna find out and it won't be here. I need to take her home and get her into bed. We're going to talk about all this shit when she wakes up, whether she wants to or not.

CHAPTER TEN

I wasn't just addicted to dope. I was addicted to self-destruction
~ Addict Chick

Angel

I'm not much of an angel. The thought circulates through my mind as I wake from the deepest sleep of my life. It's something my mother used to tell me as a child, using my name as my punishment whenever she had the opportunity. If that's not ten levels of fucked up, I don't know what is.

I rub my knuckles over my eyes and open them, seeing a very judgmental looking man sitting at my bedside. Shit. Everything starts to hit me now. I didn't go to sleep in this bed. I fell asleep at the house on my old mattress. How the hell did I get back here?

"Wanna tell me what you took?" The way he asks it is

the complete opposite of his facial expression. He isn't judging me, he's merely asking me out of concern. I've only ever had one person besides a medical professional ask me what I took, and that person has always been Pain. I just wonder why it feels so different to be asked by my brother, versus my... boyfriend? I guess that's what I call Trick. Honestly, I'm still trying to figure this shit out. There's no how-to guide for any of this. He shoots his hand out and grabs my arm, pulling it over to him. "I know you didn't shoot up, there aren't any tracks." He tells me, disapproval evident in his tone.

I try to pull my arm free of his grip, but it's no use. He's far too strong for me. Shaking my head I confess to him, much like a sinner would to a priest, "No. I didn't shoot up. I took a Xanax..." I wonder if I should ask him for his forgiveness or call him Father. I giggle at the thought of calling him that, thinking of the mere shock that would flash across his face.

He scrunches his nose, "What the fuck are you giggling about? Do you have any idea how worried I was about you?"

"I... I'm sorry. I thought of something and..." I stop talking, not even bothering to say another word. It won't do any good, and it'll just be a fuck fest.

"It's great to know that you can just think of something else and avoid the seriousness of our situation. What the fuck were you thinkin', Angel? You've been clean for weeks. What was goin' on in that mind of yours that would make you want to pop a xannie?" He releases my arm at that, pulling himself away from me. In all the time that I've known him, I've never seen him do this. Never have I witnessed him put a wall up between us. It's just showing me how upset he is with my actions.

I run my hand through my blonde hair and twirl my fingers around the ends, trying to think of the right words to say. But there aren't any, are there? "Every day I feel like I shouldn't be here," I mumble it out lowly, almost so low that I think he can't hear me. I stare down at my fingers intertwined in my locks before I continue, "I feel like I don't belong here, like I'm an outcast. I try not to feel like this, but sometimes I can't help it. I was never in this life, I was on the opposite end of the spectrum. Pain and Chaos chose to change their lives to find the sort of family here that we never had back home and I understand it. I can't blame them for it, everyone here can be great when they want to be." I smile lightly before looking up to Trick. "I don't know if you'll ever understand why I feel like this, but I'm trying to. I'm human, I have good days and I have bad ones, but just know I'm trying. I'm trying so damn hard to have the best days that I can, but today wasn't a good day."

"Yesterday," He corrects, his eyes glued to mine. "Why wasn't it a good day?"

"Elena wanted to talk to me about helping out more around here, and after we talked I told her I'd cook. So, I did cook up some stir fry, and she came back a while later and spit it out right in front of me. She didn't even swallow it, Trick. Just told me it was fucking disgusting.

It was my first real attempt at fitting in here and I was shot down in the worst way possible. Fuck! You might just think it was food, that it's something dumb to get upset about, but it wasn't just food to me. It was an opportunity to be viewed as more than just Trick's charity case druggie girlfriend." I can't help the tears that slip past my eyes. Everything I'm telling him right now is coming straight from the heart, in a way that I didn't think it would. Hell, I didn't think I'd even confess how it made me feel.

Trick grabs my hands, pressing his lips to my palms. "It's not dumb, baby. It's important to you, which means it's even more important to me. I just want you to be happy, but know that Elena told me she was havin' a bad day with her pregnancy yesterday. The baby didn't like the way it smelled. That's why she spit it out. It wasn't anythin' you did." He rises up from his seat and presses his lips softly against mine, reassuring me of my place here.

It's moments like this where I thank God that he claimed me, that it wasn't anyone else. The man can handle me at my best and at my worst, which is something that no other has ever been able to do. We may butt heads quite a bit, but we have these moments too, and I think it's well worth the occasional banter.

"Now, why'd you take the xannie?"

I sigh, "I just wanted to not feel anything. I didn't want to feel sad, but I didn't want to feel happy. I just wanted to be, and I wanted some damn good sleep."

He grumbles before I even finish what I'm saying. "You don't need drugs to help you sleep. You just need to be tired. Next time I'll make your ass run around the track until you pass out."

Furrowing my brows, I'm confused beyond belief. "What? Are you a coach or something?"

He smiles quickly before it fades, his expression turning more serious, almost as if something is haunting him. "In a past life I might have coached football. I could just fuck you, you know."

"Oh, do you want to do that? You barely have your hands on me." I tease, hoping that if I poke the bear just enough that he might just turn into a grizzly.

"Me, barely touching you?" He asks, cocking his head to the side. "Have you looked at yourself? You know how hard it is for me to behave?"

I scoff, before my laughter gets the best of me. "Not that hard, obviously. You behave all the fucking time. What do you think is going to happen if you touch me, that the sky is gonna turn black and flying monkeys will come down from the sky?"

"We just have to follow the yellow brick road, baby." He snickers, making me wanna throw my fist into his mouth.

"Asshole," I grumble.

Trick grabs the back of my hair and pulls me back against our mattress, pulling the comforter over my legs, his eyes dart up from my pussy to my eyes. "Do you want to find out what happens to bad girls who disrespect me?"

"Only if being a bad girl leads to me feeling oh so good." I taunt him, sliding my tongue out to lick my bottom lip. The bear is so close to turning into a grizzly, and by God he will.

"You're such a lil' devil." He tells me, eyes turning dark as midnight. Oh yes, I'm getting what I want.

"Nu-uh. I'm an Angel, my name says so." I flirtatiously argue, riling him up even more and more. Before I realize what's happening, he flips me over and tears off my pajama pants, slamming his hand down hard onto my ass.

"Eeeps!" I yelp out, flashing my head back up to him. "What was that for?!"

"You being a smart ass brat."

"Seriously? You like my sassy mouth. Don't tell me you don't." He lands his hand on my ass again, this time even harder than before. The stinging sensation radiates through my cheek. "Jesus! What in the actual fuck? Obviously you like it when I get this way. I see Peter the pecker getting hard as we speak, waiting to go to pound town with Paula the pussy!" I hiss-yell at him.

"You're fuckin' crazy, namin' your private parts."

"I named yours too, but obviously you didn't notice that."

Stinging meets my ass yet again. "Jesus!" I yell at him, somehow managing to fenagle my pants off my legs. I'm just in a soft pink thong, with a gray cami shirt. Never have I been this exposed to him before. "If you want Paula so much, just take her." Spreading my legs, I cock my eyebrow and stare up at him.

His hand shoots up to my throat as his grip tightens around me. Fingers constricting my airway, he smirks before his lips are pressing against my ear. A low grumble greets me before the sound of his voice follows, "Let's get one thing straight. I don't want Paula, I want Angel and I'm gonna get every single part." Trick releases my neck and grabs my hips, pulling me down to his torso. I don't know how the hell I didn't notice he freed his cock from his jeans, but I feel him pressing against my entrance. "Now's the chance to back out, baby. It's gonna hurt."

"Yeah, right. There's no way –" I stop immediately at the feel of him shoving his cock inside of me. It's like trying to squeeze an oversized butternut squash up there! "Relax, your body knows what to do." He whispers in a soothing tone, easing in and out of me. I'm soaking wet, biting the bottom of my lip as he rocks himself inside. The pain slowly transforms into pleasure, making me feel at ease.

"You were sayin'?" He teases, and I roll my eyes at him. I move my hand to his beard, yanking him down closer to me, needing the taste of his lips on mine. There's never been a moment like this in my entire life, where I feel like I'm not alone. Trick makes me feel so much but most of all, he makes me feel *alive*. As though I've never lived before.

"Jesus," I mutter out a groan, smirking up at the man who never ceases to surprise me. He accepts me for everything I am, flaws and quirks. Turns pain into pleasure, so I wonder if there's anything that he can't do.

I rise up, pulling my cami free from my body and let my tits fall in front of his face. I won't ask him what I want him to do, because I beg for no man. He'll get the message, though.

His tongue rolls out over my flesh, gliding along my collarbone before dipping down over my breasts. Sucking one nipple into his mouth and then the other, he goes back and forth as his pace quickens inside my pussy.

I throw my head back as my breathing quickens, "Good God, Trick!" He might have a monster of a cock, but he sure knows how to use it.

"You have no idea just how long I've wanted to hear that come from your lips."

I counter back to him, opening up my heart, body and soul just a bit more. "And you probably don't know how long I've wanted to."

"You are a fuckin' Angel, and you don't even see it."

"We both know I'm not." He can say it as much as he wants, but I'm nowhere near as sweet as he thinks I am.

"You are. You're *my* Angel."

"Fuck!" I scream out, clenching the sheets to our bed. His cock hit me in just the right spot, my orgasm rolling over me in a series of waves. He pounds his cock into me over and over again so fast I can hear the gush of cum coming out of me. Not stopping, he continues for a good few minutes until he growls out like an uncaged animal.

The door to our room flies open, "Are you Oo-. OH MY GOD!" I don't know whose voice that just was... but I find it hysterical that we were just walked in on.

I laugh like I haven't in years and look up to the man whose holding me in his arms, monster cock still nestled deep inside me. "Do I wanna know who that was?"

He shrugs, "Daisy. I'm wonderin' what she's more shocked about, the fact half my cock is still out of you, or that she saw me pounding your pretty cunt."

"A combination of both no doubt." I chuckle, glancing between us to see the bastard isn't fucking with me. He can win a world record for biggest dick, both thick and long.

Jesus. It'll be fun playing with his Peter.

CHAPTER ELEVEN

Karma doesn't spare anyone
~ IdeaSpot

Trick

"We've all been preparing for this for weeks. All of you know your roles, and you know that even though we hate the bastard, keeping him alive is our job. After he's sold is another story," Reed tells us, adding a wink on the last bit. Today is a day we have been waiting on for quite a while. The day of Rafael's auction and shit I can't wait for this.

We all arrived here a couple of hours ago, conducting perimeter checks, ensuring that no one tried to fuck with anything, checking for bombs. That kinda shit. Honestly, I was a bit surprised when not a hair was out of place. I didn't expect that. Then again, everyone wants to buy this bastard, so they can conduct their own torture on him.

Dmitri arrived a few minutes ago and met both Chaos and I in the middle of the hotel's ballroom. The entire place has been redecorated and reconstructed to fit the needs of tonight's event. In the middle of the room, Rafael is chained on a concrete pedestal with a collar around his neck. The only way he is able to break free of it is by unlocking himself, using the key that Mariana Petran holds in her possession. After he is sold, Mariana will give the key to the highest bidder to do whatever it is that they wish.

"This has been a long time coming. Rafael had done some shit to the Vipers MC, back before we patched over into the Skulls Renegade. He always has been and always will be a disgusting human being. I can't wait for someone to buy him and give him what he deserves." Dmitri speaks with disgust lacing his voice, and even goes as to so much as turn, spitting on Rafael. The glare that he gets in return is useless. Rafael won't be breaking free, not in the slightest. Truthfully, I would've spit on him first if Dmitri hadn't. The man deserves no respect.

Two of Mariana and Ion Petran's team are at the entryway of the ballroom, and another two are around the corner in case anyone were to attempt to try to get in through the back doors. They're locked, but when push comes to shove, people know how to break in. The thought process of placing security at the auction was a grueling task. We need a combination of both Skulls and mafia men throughout the surrounding area.

The double doors open, and five people come walking in. I recognize Reed and Elena immediately, and it takes me a moment to notice Mariana and Ion. But I don't know who the older gentleman is who entered with them. He smiles to both the Romanian King and Queen, shaking both of their hands before walking in our direction.

"Pleasant day, isn't it lads?" He greets us, lowering his gaze to Rafael. "I'm betting the lot of you don't know much about who I am. Do ya?"

"No, Sir." I reply, not knowing where the Sir comes from. Assumption, probably. He came walkin' in with the two power couples which tells me that he's just as important as them.

"Doesn't surprise me in the least bit. I don't have too much business over on this side of the pond. I'm Desmond Mackenzie, Irish Mafia." Did this dude really just introduce himself like he's James Bond? It sure as fuck felt like he did. I try not to laugh, wanting to show respect to the old man, but shit, it's hard to keep this one tucked down.

"You seem to have gotten yourself in quite the bit of trouble now, haven't ya Rafael?"

Rafael mumbles something out. It's no use, though. He has a red ball gag in his mouth, prepped and ready to be someone's bitch. Who'd want to listen to this motherfucker anyway?

"You see here boys, Rafael is my wife's brother. He's obviously the sour one of the bunch and I've never been able to prove the things he's done against me and my children... but I am no fool. Some would assume I'd be here to help you, you poor idiot. But instead I will be here to shake hands with the person who buys you like the overused heifer you are. I can't wait until you go to slaughter. Lord knows you deserve it for every atrocity you've committed."

Rafael continues trying to mumble, thrashing his body towards his brother-in-law but it's no use. He's on his knees, tied down so securely that all he can do is thrash his body a little bit to the right or left. Not much else he can do. "Oh, Rafael. Are you trying to say something? I can't hear you." I'm beginning to like this old bastard more and more with each growing moment. He's giving Rafael what he deserves.

Out of nowhere I see Desmond grab Rafael by the back of the head and my gun is drawn, trained on him. "Let go of the prisoner, lucky charms."

"Oh, relax. I'm not going to kill him. I'm merely having a bit of fun before we begin." He states, as if that will change what I've just said.

I sigh, looking over to both Dmitri and Chaos who both shrug. "I won't repeat myself. Back it up."

He rips his fist away from Rafael's head and as he opens his fist, a clump of hair falls free. Gross. Desmond glances back to Rafael, giving him a look that I know very well. It's obvious these two don't have a normal family relationship. Desmond might have said he isn't going to kill him, but it doesn't mean that he doesn't want to. "You're the reason she's in a coma. I know that in my heart, and for all these years I've wondered why you would do this to her. Of why your actions would have led her to a place like this. She has been suffering all of these years because of *you*."

I glimpse towards the door and see that the room now has at least fifty, if not sixty people in it. It's funny how your surroundings can drastically change when you're focused on something.

"It's go time, brothers. Game faces on."

CHAPTER TWELVE

Never underestimate the power of intuition. I know your game
before you even play it
~ LittleNivi

Trick

"Thank you all so much for attending this evening. I know that you have each travelled from great distances, so I'll save us some time and hop straight to it." Mariana speaks into a microphone, her voice echoing through the entire ballroom, calling everyone into a round of silence. "Rafael Ramirez is finally where he belongs, chained to the floor like the rabid animal he is. Unlogical. Blood-thirsty. Power-hungry. These are the three traits that this supposed leader has, and ultimately they are the three things that led to his demise. His rap-sheet is long, and while most would commend him for that. I am confident that no one in this room will. We're all here for one reason, because Rafael has harmed each and every one of us in some way. I will ask this, though. How is it that a room filled with some of the most powerful people in the world, we were unable to cage this monster? That is something that we can simply never allow to happen again. We all might not get along from time to time because of our business dealings, but we are businessmen and women, nonetheless. I would like to formally welcome Francisco Lopez as the newly reigning Cartel leader. I hope that we can have a fruitful business relationship." Ion takes his stance next to his wife, so late in her speech. It shocks me a bit, considering the Romanians are a generation or two behind women equality. From what I understand, the men hold all the power.

There's a quick movement to my left, and I see the shimmer of a blade heading in one direction – towards Rafael. I see the woman who wields it and decide not to pull out my Glock. Instead, I grab her by the wrist and fling her so hard she doesn't know what to do. The knife falls to the floor, and she has an obvious case of whiplash as her ass hits the ground. "What the hell were you thinkin'?" I ask her, not understanding how she could be so stupid. She can't be older than her early twenties. Her skin looks so soft, telling me she is young, but her eyes show so much pain.

She refuses to look at me, glaring eyes looking straight at Rafael. "He raped my sister and then slit her throat in our home. My father did nothing. He refused to get justice for her. This man breathes air every day while my sister is in the ground. It isn't right." I can't argue with her. It isn't right, but what she's doing is not the right way.

"Listen, kid. Life's a bitch and nothing ever works out the way we want it to. Today, I can assure you this motherfucker will die. But you just have to be patient. Your sister wouldn't want you to die from attempting to avenge her. You have a hell of a lot to live for, so live. Don't just live for you, live for your sister, too." Ion has witnessed the entire ordeal I just de-escalated, and I'm waiting to see what he wants me to do. All he does is stares in my direction, so I wave my hand up towards one of the mafia goons to come over and grab the girl. At my signal, one comes walking right over and once he's in front of me I speak. "Take the girl out of here and make sure she doesn't regain entry."

"Let's get this started, shall we?" Ion says, the roaring of the crowd behind him. "We'll start this auction at three million dollars. All of the proceeds from this sale will be split amongst many charities, primarily focusing in sexual and domestic abuse, human trafficking, and cancer centers."

A group of men and women come to stand before Ion, all holding signs with numbers on them to place their bid. "Do I have anyone for three million?" Several bidders raise their numbers at his question, and the process continues over and over again until he's well over twenty-four million. It's astonishing to see what price one head can hold.

I keep my eyes focused on my surroundings, looking for any sort of imminent threat but am pleased when I don't see anyone else attempt what that dumb, young girl did. She was lucky to leave here with her life. Everyone in this room seems dead set on causing a shit ton of harm to Rafael, and I don't blame them for that. Bastard deserves everything that's coming to him.

As more minutes quickly pass, the crowd in front of Ion starts to slowly diminish. Each meeting their limit. "Thirty-three million?" Ion states, looking to the three people who stand before him. An Asian woman holds the number thirty-seven, A tall red-headed man holds the number seventy-two and a short blonde woman is holding the number fifty-two. The Asian girl smirks, raising her number and I think she's pretty sure she has this, but the blonde girl raises hers quickly, "Thirty-seven million." She offers.

The man shakes his head and backs away, leaving these two eager women to bid for their bosses.

I see Mariana staring down at the Asian girl and if I'm seein' this shit it sure as fuck means everyone else is. This Romanian Queen is smart, I'll give her that. "Forty-seven million," The Asian girl counters, giving a bit of side eye to the blonde bitch beside her.

Shit, we might even have a good old cat fight tonight too.

The blonde girl takes a visible gulp, a slight bit of fear

crossing over her face. She doesn't know what to do, whether to keep going or stop it now.

"Going once, going twice, sold to number thirty-seven!" The auction had used private bidders, no one wanting to show themselves to their opposition. I completely understand that, and can only imagine how high he would have gone for if that was the case.

Mariana takes the microphone from Ion's hand and begins speaking, "I am the proud new owner of Rafael Ramirez, as Jing-Lee was bidding on my behalf." The crowd begins to speak up, shocked at what she's done. But how can they be shocked by her actions? She's a woman who obviously doesn't stand up for any bullshit.

"This whole thing was rigged, wasn't it?!" A man shouts out from the corner.

She cackles into the microphone, "No, it most certainly was not. If it was, none of you would have been provided with ample opportunity to outbid me. Quit being a sore loser, will you, Fredrik?"

Ion chuckles, but then shoots his wife a warning glare.

"She's right you know." Desmond tells Fredrik, "We were all given the opportunity to out-bid her and none of us did. The only person we can blame for that is ourselves."

"Bastards." Fredrik shouts in a state of pure anger. "You have no power, Mariana. We all know who does and that's your husband. Who's to say that your bid is even valid?"

Mariana's expression shifts into something I've never seen before, she's obviously offended but the smile that crosses her face means nothing good. "I am. Anything my wife does, has my backing. What I will not tolerate, and never will is someone who thinks that she deserves the type of disrespect you have just bestowed upon her." Ion raises his hand in the air and the next thing everyone knows, his men are coming for Fredrik, dragging him by his arms away from the ballroom and out through the double doors.

"Please continue, love." He tells his wife.

"With pleasure," She comments back. "Rafael will not leave this place alive. I will guarantee you all that, and before you moan and groan about that fact, know that you will each have a part in his death. For it's not just my right, he has done so much to all of us."

The doors open to the ballroom and some sort of device is bought in, it's wooden and is being rolled in multiple parts. Before my very eyes, I watch as it's put together piece by piece, looking like some sort of medivel torture device.

It's some sort of wooden triangle, with chains that come down from the top. On each side holds a metal clasp, with more chains. Mariana obtains the key and walks over towards us, unlocking Rafael. "Please position him properly, will you?" She asks her men, and they do as they're told within a few minutes.

His hands are positioned above his head, wrapped securely in chains. He's already trying to move them, but it's no use as he only moves a centimeter or two at best. I'll admit, Mariana did a good job of planning this far. Each of his legs are grabbed and shackled to the wood. Chains secure every limb he has, and I think it's safe to say that there's no way he's getting out of this. "Continue, please." She states to one of her men, who grabs a knife and puts the blade against Rafael's clothes, ripping everything off of him, so he's exposed to the entire room.

Another man comes forward holding two black buckets and sets them on the left and right of the contraption. I take a look down into the bucket and see knives. "In front of Rafael you will see two buckets filled with knives. I encourage you all to take a step forward and grab a knife. Please stand in a singular line and as you approach him, cut him, wherever you'd like. No stabbing will be allowed. But don't fret, the fun will begin a bit later."

Desmond Mackenzie is the first to form the line, grabbing a knife he approaches his brother-in-law and slashes the blade against his face. Stepping away, there's a cut from the top of his head through his lip. A jagged groan is all we hear in response. I'd much rather have it this way, to not be subjected to hearing his bitchin' and moanin'.

"Tell me there's gonna be more than cutting him..." Chaos mumbles angrily, repositioning himself beside me. Dmitri does the same, crossing his arms and stares at Rafael.

"Of course there will." Dmitri tells him, "What she's

doing is good. Giving him death by a thousand cuts, one of the oldest forms of torture in history."

"Yeah, *right*." Chaos doesn't believe anything of what Dmitri's just said. "What she's doing is good, hmm?"

"She's making him suffer, and this is just the tip of the iceberg. Be patient." I tell Chaos, hoping my words will ease his angered mind.

Over the matter of a few hours men and women come back for third and forth opportunities to mark Rafael's skin with a blade. His groans and mumbles of pain turning into sounds only a wounded animal would make. If he thinks that any of us will feel sorry for him, he's sadly mistaken.

"Thank you all for your contribution in today's event. If you'd like to stay to see how Rafael's life comes to its very late end, please do. If not, you know how to exit." Mariana says to the crowd through the microphone. A few people decide to leave, while the rest opt to stay and witness what has been long overdue.

Blood is oozing over his skin, some of it wet, some of it dried from the older cuts that have been open for more than a couple of hours. From the corner of my eye I see three girls walk in, one of them I immediately recognize. "I didn't know Maria was showing up," I say to Chaos, who throws his head over in her direction.

He grumbles out his response, "Neither did I."

"Who are those two women with her? I've never seen them before." I say, able to tell that Maria knows them because she's chatting to the both of them. The group of them walk up to Elena, the black girl, gives her a hug first, placing her hand on Elena's huge stomach and then the smaller girl with the long hair does the same.

"That's Cecil and Kimberley. They were all trafficked by Rafael together. When Elena was working with the FBI to crack trafficking down in an attempt to nab Rafael for all his shit, she and Reed purchased a few girls. Maria, Cecil and Kimberley were the first of many."

Damn. I had no fucking clue.

"Is Elena still working for the FBI?" I ask, not really knowing too much about her past.

"Eh. If she is, none of us know about it." Chaos says.

Dmitri shrugs. "I don't think she is. I think both of them use each other as resources when they can, but she hasn't involved herself in their matters for a while. Especially now since the baby is coming."

Chaos huffs, "They sure keep hush about this shit."

"Sure do. But not our job to worry about it." I tell him.

The three girls walk straight towards Rafael and by God they seem to be a force to be reckoned with. The girl with the long hair, or Kimberley as Chaos just told me says something lowly to Rafael. I can only hear the mumbling of words before I see her grab a knife and shove that fucker straight into his micro-dick. Jesus! I don't feel sorry for him or anything in the slightest, but that was hard to watch.

"I've been waitin' a long ass time for this day to come. Just glad I could be here to witness it." Cecil says to him, digging her blade up from his middle finger, along his forearm, over his shoulder and to his neck. She's gone over countless open wounds, cutting deeper than anyone else had before her. His eyes grow wide at the pain that is obviously flooding his body as he cries out through the gag.

She steps away, and then I see Maria, with a somber look across her face. She's paler than usual, as if the sight of him physically makes her nauseous. Cecil heads towards a bag that is close to Mariana, both of them saying a few short words before she returns, opening it in front of Maria. "Whatever she's doing, you don't interrupt." I tell Chaos, looking over to him. "This is her retribution, not yours."

"I have a right to participate, to make him suffer."

"No, you fuckin' don't. This is for her, not you so keep your selfish ass back here or Dmitri and I will make sure you do." I hiss out, not understanding how he isn't grasping the importance of whatever it is Maria is going to do. This is her closure for everything that has been done to her. I'm not even her ol'man and I see that.

Maria digs her knife into his chest, peeling back the layer of skin until she reaches muscle. She inserts her knife even further, smiling when his screams grow louder. "I don't think you've realized what I'm doing yet, but you will. I don't know how yours is still beating after all these years. After you've proven to everyone countless times that you don't have one. So, it's simple. I'm going to rip it out of you."

His eyes go wider than I've ever seen them, and I

snicker. Bastard is getting what he fuckin' deserves. Cecil pulls out some sort of saw from the bag and hands it to Maria. It's small and compact, so I'm sure she'll be able to use it.

She clicks a button, and at that the machine comes to life. Over the sound of the motor, she yells at him. "I have to get through your ribcage first, but if you pass out, don't worry. I have something that will wake you right up!"

"Jesus Christ. Remind me to never piss her off..." Chaos says, getting a chuckle from Dmitri.

The sound of the saw hitting the bone greets us. Shocking me at how similar, it sounds to sawing down a tree. With every rib she's going through, I can almost hear the resemblance of a tree limb breaking.

The crowd begins to chatter, probably talking about how fuckin' crazy this Latina bitch is. Can't blame them for that.

Suddenly, the saw turns off and the sounds of Rafael's screaming greets us. Maria smiles proudly, "I don't feel sorry for you one bit, not after everything you've done to us all. You deserve every bit of what you're getting." She places her hand against his chest and picks at the loose bones, pulling them back towards her, something almost carcass like falls from his body. I'm no doctor, and I sure as fuck don't want to be after seein' this shit.

Groans and screams continue to come from him until his head falls to his chest. "Jude!" Maria shouts, calling Purgatory's doctor over.

He comes walking up with a vile of something in his hands. He opens it, rubs it along his finger and then under Rafael's nose. "Give it a moment and he'll wake right back up." He tells her, approaching us.

She stands there, bloodied arms crossed.

"Did you know how crazy your bitch is?" He asks Chaos, who responds in a glare. "Okay, nevermind."

Rafael shifts his head to the left and the right in a circular motion, coming back to us. "There you are! I couldn't have you missing the grand finale."

He mutters something into his ballgag in response, so Mariana unclasps it, allowing it to fall and hit the ground. "What was that you were saying?"

His eyes are filled with exhaustion, but a callousness lies behind them. Even when knocked down, he is still a savage beast. "You'll burn in hell for this, girl."

Maria laughs, digging her hand inside of him. "I've already been to hell and back." She pulls her hand back hard and I witness her ripping his heart straight from his chest cavity, tossing it on the floor behind her. "Like I said, you shouldn't have one of these." Maria doesn't so much as look at anyone while she makes her way for the front door.

Jesus, I never thought this is how today would've gone.

CHAPTER THIRTEEN

Don't force yourself to fit in where you don't belong
~ JustLiveHappy

Angel

"Fuck, she did *what?!*" Enzo shouts into his phone. I don't know who he's talking to but I'm assuming it's one of the guys. Today was the auction for that evil dude. I walk towards him, giving him a concerned look. Out of everyone here, Enzo is the last to judge me, and I'd like to think that because of that we're friends. He hangs up and tosses his phone on the pool table. "Jesus!"

I raise my eyebrows at him, "Care to elaborate on what's so shocking?"

He stands up, eyes going wide if I've ever seen such a thing. "Maria ripped his fucking heart out of his chest."

"Huh?" I'm confused. There's no way he could've just said what he did.

"Maria cut his skin, carved off his muscle, took a fuckin' bone saw to his ass and cut out his ribs and then she dug her hand up in there and ripped out his heart."

Good God. My insides are rolling. "There's no way she would've done something like that." I say, not wanting to believe it. Cause if she did... it means she's one twisted bitch.

"She did." He firmly states as I try to wrap my head around it.

I thought I heard her come in through the back a bit ago, so I leave the main room in the clubhouse and head to the back towards her room. I hit my hand against the door a couple times, and with no answer I decide to just let myself in. As I open the door, I see Maria sitting on the edge of her bed, her body wrapped in a towel with her hair dangling over her side.

We aren't really friends, but we're friendly to one another. She's essentially my sister-in-law, so I should check in with her. It's the right thing to do. "Maria, are you okay?" I ask because I'm genuinely concerned, especially at what Enzo just told me she did. It's not normal for someone to act like that.

"I'm nowhere near close to being okay." She mutters, staring down at the floor. "I don't know how to be okay right now."

I take a couple steps towards her and sit next to her on the bed. "What's the matter?"

She laughs at first, but then it turns into a heartfelt sobbing cry. "Everything is. Every part of everything."

"You're not making any sense…" I tell her lowly, not wanting to sound judgmental or rude.

"I missed my period and took a pregnancy test last week. It was positive. I didn't tell either of your brothers and I don't know how the fuck I'm supposed to tell them this."

I smile, knowing that they're going to be so happy with this news. "You just tell them, Maria. They are going to love hearing this from you!"

She shakes her head back and forth, "No, they won't. They'll hate this. They'll hate it. They'll hate me." At this point I wrap my arms around her and pull her to my chest as her sobs grow heavier. I don't understand why she feels this way.

"They won't hate that baby at all, they will love and adore it more than anything else in this entire world, and God help anyone who tries to fuck with your bundle of joy."

"Torment, bundle of torment." I don't think I'm hearing her right. "There is nothing joyous about having your rapist's baby."

Oh. My. God.

"Maria, it'll be okay. It will. I promise you…" I'm making promises that will never be able to be kept, promising her that everything will be okay in the end when we already know the possibility of that happening is slim to none.

She whips her head in my direction, looking up at me with tear filled eyes. "Please don't tell anyone. Please, Angel. I can't. No one can know about this, not even Trick. I need this to stay in our family, because if I decide to… keep it… I don't want anyone looking at it at feeling sorry for it, or for me. I can't live with the shame of knowing everyone else knows… please keep this secret. I'm begging you, please."

"You don't have to worry. I won't say a word. I promise, I won't ever say a word." This isn't my secret to tell, but I know firsthand how secrets can end up killing you. I just hope it doesn't for her sake.

I hope this burden won't be too hard to bare.

CHAPTER FOURTEEN

Why fit in when you were born to stand out?
~ Dr. Seuss

Angel

It's been three days since Maria confessed to me that her baby is fathered by Rafael, the now deceased ex-leader of the Mexican Cartel, also known as her rapist. Truthfully, it hurts my heart to know about the turmoil she must be going through every single day. The thoughts that must be running through her mind. I'm not even sure if she's told either of my brothers yet, but it's not my place to say anything. I've kept my promise, though, I haven't told a soul. Not even Trick.

It's the end of February at this point and with that the weather is starting to get a bit warmer. I can't fucking wait for spring, to feel the air blowing against my face as

Trick takes me for a ride on his bike. Pfft, he hasn't even asked me to. I'm just assuming that he will at some point.

"You're still here?" Immediately I'm able to identify the bitch whose voice is speaking to me. I turn around and look at her, still not understanding why she hates me so much.

I roll my eyes and sigh, cause' lord knows she will still not grasp this even after I say it again. "I'm not going anywhere."

"You need to. Preferably back on the streets and keep yourself far away from the club. We can't have you ruining shit for us, Angel. That's always what happens with you. Everything you touch turns to ash. You're an infection, ruining everything for everyone."

Here we go, *again*.

I turn to face her as my entire body fills with anger that I've never felt before. "Listen up, Jenna. I don't know why the fuck you have a constant stick up your ass whenever I'm around, but you need to lose it. I'm not going anywhere. In fact, I'm staying right where I am with the man who happens to adore me, so either get used to it or don't bother coming around at all."

"You don't know why I have a stick up my ass? Are you dumb? Do you not remember what *you* made her do!?" I want to ask her if this bitch has lost her damn mind. I have no idea what she's talking about, not in the slightest bit.

"What are you talking about!?" I scream at her, throwing my hands up in the air.

She grabs me by the back of my hair and yanks my head down, glaring at me right in the eyes. "You don't remember me when we were younger. Do you?"

I squint my eyes together, pushing my hands against her to try to get her to let me go. Luckily, after a second time with a good bit of force behind me, she does. "What the hell is that supposed to mean?"

"I was on the streets too, for a time. You and I crossed the same paths a time or two," There's no way. I would remember a girl like Jenna. "Do you remember Dot?" Immediately when she says the name, I remember the girl. Dot was a girl who was trying to get off the streets, off drugs. It didn't work well for her. She died after she got mixed up with a dealer who was giving out a bad batch of something. I don't think any of us will ever know the full story.

"What about her?"

Jenna looks flabbergasted. "Holy shit. You don't remember. You don't remember any of it! You introduced her to Troy, you piece of shit. You're the reason she's dead!" Her voice rises and she lunges straight at me, knocking me down onto the ground. She pulls her fist back and before I can move my head, her knuckles come plummeting down into my face.

"You're crazy!" I shout, moving my hands up to block my face.

I hear a scream from another direction and see Elena walking towards us, "What is this madness? Get off of her, Jenna!" Elena orders Jenna, but she doesn't listen.

Instead, she slams her fist into my nose, and I feel blood flow over my lips and into my mouth. "That's it!" Elena hollers, and I see her figure walking towards us. She grabs Jenna by the shoulder and the next thing I know, she goes down. Jenna didn't touch her, and obviously I didn't either.

"Elena!?" I worriedly call out her name, moving my body quickly and cause Jenna to lose her grounding. She falls to her ass on the floor next to me as I crawl towards Elena. Her hands are on her belly and she looks like she's in a fuck ton of pain. "We have to get her to the hospital now!" I tell Jenna, because I can't do this alone. It doesn't matter if we don't get along. The only thing that matters is making sure that Elena and the baby are okay.

CHAPTER FIFTEEN

Your only limit is your mind
~ Lillaliptak.com

Trick

We got a text from Michelle saying that Angel, Jenna and Elena were at the hospital. She didn't know why, and she only knew because she got a text from Jenna. I'm just chargin' through these fuckin' hallways wonderin' why the fuck they didn't text their men this shit. The three of them better know that they're gonna be in a world of shit when we get to them. Thank fuck Michelle knew to message the Skulls Renegade group chat to let us know what was going on. Somehow, I was the first one through the doors and charged straight up to the nurse's station.

"Hey lady, I'm lookin' for a couple girls. One's blonde with long hair, the other is a super pregnant redhead and the last has dark hair with a load of tattoos." I say to the nurse who's typing away on her computer.

She looks up at me through her glasses and furrows her brows, bringing her hand up slowly to take them off of the bridge of her nose and set them around her bosom. "How am I supposed to know who you're looking for, mister? You have a name or something that is actually helpful?"

Before I can even think, I spit out a name. "Elena Michaels,"

She types the name in the computer and nods, "You her family or something?"

I nod, "Yep. I'm her older brother. She's pregnant and we got a message saying she was in the hospital with my girlfriend and a family friend. Do you have any information on them?" I ask, thinking I've made some leeway with this lady.

"Brother, hmm?" Every bit of her tone tells me that she's calling me out on my horseshit. She's seein' right through it and that isn't helping me none. "Candi. Does this look like Elena's brother to you?" She shouts back to another nurse who's scrolling away on a tablet. The woman looks up, eying me up and down.

The new nurse chuckles lowly, shaking her head back and forth. "Care to pull out your identification, Sir?"

I grab my wallet from the back of my jeans and pull out my driver's license, handing it over to the woman. Oh, if she wants to play this game, we will *play*. "We have different last names. Different dads."

I hear the clanking of combat boots and look down the hallway to see Reed charging my way, with Dmitri in tow not far behind him. As soon as he gets to the nurse's station he slams his hands on the counter, obviously out of breath from his run. "Candi. Where is my wife?" He completely bypasses the rude old woman in front of me.

"Room 105. Glad to see you." Reed doesn't even reply, darting away to where I can only imagine is Elena's room.

The old woman clicks her tongue at me as her sights land on Dmitri. "Now *that* is Elena's brother. Don't you ever try to lie to me, mister, or I'll shove a scalpel somewhere it doesn't belong."

Dmitri puts his hand around the back of my neck and laughs, "Oh, don't pay him any mind Mildred. He's just a concerned brother."

She huffs and rolls her eyes, "You boys drive me insane with your brother bullshit. You aren't all brothers. If you were, I'd feel real sorry for your momma. Please explain to your *brother* the hospital's policies on what classifies as a blood relative."

Dmitri and I walk together down the hallway, "What room did she say?" He asks.

"105," I reply, before turning to look at him. "She said you were Elena's brother. What's that bat been smokin'?"

"It's complicated, but Elena and I are family. Her father adopted me when I was a kid." He says it slowly, almost as if telling me this fact about him hurts. He's not the type of man to show emotion, and I can't blame him for that. I'm not the light and fluffy kinda guy either. I'd rather just keep it build up inside and deal with my inner demons where they belong – trapped in my dungeon of a body.

"How did I not know that shit?" I mean to ask my question internally, but it slips out.

He shrugs as we walk up to room 105. "It's not really something we talk about. Stirs up a lot of old shit, a lot of old memories that neither one of us want to relive. The past doesn't matter. The only thing that does is the now, and our future. No point in thinking about the past."

"Trick," Angel's voice is soft, and sounds like it's filled with fear. I glance over her way, seeing her standing on the other side of the room. Her arms are wrapped around her body, staying a few feet away from Elena in the hospital bed and from Jenna who is sitting in the chair, holding Elena's hand.

Even staring at my girl, I know something is wrong. Call it intuition, but something is wrong here. I move my hand up and motion for her to come over, and she does, quicker than she ever has since we've been together. Her small frame runs into my body like a ton of bricks, arms wrapping around my waist. She buries her head into my chest, and I run my hand along the back of her head, tangling my fingers in her hair, giving a shit attempt at soothing her.

"What happened?" I ask, keeping my voice low as I take her a couple feet away from the door and direct her towards the waiting area. When Dmitri and I passed by it, I saw that there was no one there. Hopefully, it's the same way we just left it. I'd like some privacy while I talk to her. If there isn't any, she might not open up.

Her voice comes out in a hushed whisper, "Jenna and I got into a fight at the club. Elena tried to break it up and then she just... I don't know. We knew something was wrong, so we got her to the hospital as quick as we could."

I take a step back from Angel, pulling her from my embrace and take a good look at her. She and Jenna got into a fight, and I know better than to think no fists were drawn or hair was pulled. Seein' her lips tell me that I'm exactly right. Her lip is split wide open, not to mention the bruised nose she has. I graze my finger over her bloody wound, "Jenna do this?"

She places her finger on her lips and squints her eyes, "I didn't even know about this one."

"Shit." I mutter. I grab my cell from the back of my pants and realize I didn't get my license back from that old bat Mildred, so I go and grab it from her. In the meantime, I'm texting Enzo and asking his ass to come pick up Angel and take her back to the club. I need to make sure someone's eyes are on her while I handle an errand. But first, I need to deal with something even more pressing.

"Sweetheart, can you sit right here, for me?"

She nods her head, and I walk back over to the nurses' station and get her an ice packet. Before I go unleash my wrath, I hand it to Angel. "Hold that against your nose and lip, baby. Enzo is coming here to take you back home. I want you to take some Advil and then go straight to bed. I have to run an errand and I'll be a while."

"Okay," At her response, I turn on my heel and walk straight back to room 105. I have a bone to pick, and it won't be an easy one. My anger is overflowing inside me and there's nothing I can do about it. I propel straight towards the only person who will ensure this shit comes to an end. Dmitri is standing behind Jenna, and by the way my nostrils are flaring, I'm pretty sure he knows why I'm upset.

I take a couple steps in the room, directing my attention to Elena first. "How you feelin', momma?"

She shrugs her shoulders, offering a small smile. "Eh, okay I guess. I'll be better when they tell me what's going on with our little muffin here."

"Okay, well if you need anything you just holler, you hear?"

"Yep, Trick. I will. Thank you."

I turn my attention to Dmitri, "I mean no disrespect, especially bein' in the presence of Elena and Reed while they're dealin' with this shit, but I'll say this once. Get your bitch on a leash. I'm tired of the way she treats Angel and I won't keep putting up with this senseless bullshit. Bein' at the club is hard enough on her, and Jenna throwing insults and punches isn't helping. The club is Angel's home now," I glare right at Jenna as I say this last bit, needing it to sink into her thick fuckin' skull. "Get the fuck over it!"

At that, I leave and go handle some shit that is urgent. Or a death sentence, I'm not really sure which. I guess I'll find out when I get there.

CHAPTER SIXTEEN

The past is a place of reference, not a place of residence
~ Allcupation.com

Trick

I got a text from an anonymous number six days ago, telling me to meet someone here at this gas station, in the middle of bumfuck nowhere. Looking around, I don't see anything for miles besides this joint. Some sort of old, mom and pop gas station that probably did pretty good back in the day.

It's startin' to get a little warmer as of late and thank God for that. I would hate to have been standin' out here three weeks ago when it was so cold it made you realize that men have nipples too. I take a look at my phone and see its twenty minutes past the designated time that this meet was supposed to happen. Fuck, I don't even know what this meet was for in the first place. But, for some reason my gut was tellin' me that I needed to be here. My gut has never treated me wrong before, so of course I'd be trustin' it now.

I inspect the area one last time and decide to say fuck this shit and go inside this gas station. I doubt whoever the bastard was who texted me would just leave me hangin'. There has to be something around here somewhere. I push myself off my bike and walk towards the old building, head towards the front door and place my hand on the metal handle. A loud creaking sound greets me as I pull it forward, the age of this place showing.

Darkness greets me, even though it's sunny outside. I bring up the flashlight on my phone and illuminate the surrounding area. My eyes land on something that I could never see coming. Something that destroys me, bit by bit.

Blonde hair.

Blood.

Bodies.

It's the same three things, taped up all over this entire joint.

I can't fully allow myself to fathom, whose bodies I'm staring at. It would be way too much. It would bring back too many bad memories. My eyes catch the glimmer of something different on the back wall of this place. Not wanting to look at the photographs of my murdered family members, I approach the oddity in the room. On the wall, in red it reads 'vengeance will come'.

Make no mistake, I know who's behind this. The same people who are responsible for my family's death. This just means two things, that they're still around and the confirmation that I'll finally have my chance at getting the retribution I deserve. The bastards who did this know I'm out... which can be a good or a bad thing. It means they're getting sloppy, especially doin' some amateur shit like this.

So many emotions roll through my body like a fast train, flying over the tracks. I think I know a bit, but the reality is that I don't know too much. The only thing I really know is that I can't be here right now. I can't fuckin' breathe, and I need to get out. I have to get the fuck out of here!

I rush out of the front door of the gas station and much to my surprise, the contents in my stomach come hurling out of my body. I'm not a man who is easily made sick by things such as this, but when you know the people in the photographs, the way they'd laugh or joke. The way my nephews hated sunny-side up eggs, and how my sister refused to eat chocolate cake because it's not as pretty as red velvet... it fucks with you.

I look back at my phone and see a text from Enzo. Sliding it open, I read.

Your girl didn't wanna leave until she knew what's going on with Elena. I'm still here with her.

I text him back quickly,

Okay. I'll be there in twenty minutes. Stay put.

It sure didn't take me twenty minutes to get there. I don't know if it's the adrenaline rushing through my veins, or just the fact I want to get as far away from the ugliness of my past that I can. Either way, I'm here.

"Hey," I say to my girl, who's sitting next to Enzo with her arms drawn across her chest.

Angel doesn't even smile when she sees me, which is something that's turned into our norm. I sneak a quick kiss on her cheek, not wanting to irritate her lip. "How's my girl?"

"I'm okay, I guess. I'm worried about Elena and the baby. Reed said she's having contractions..."

Contractions? That kid still has to cook for a few more weeks. "What do you mean she's having contractions? Isn't it too early for that kid to come out?"

Angel rolls her eyes, "You are such a chimp, acting like you don't know how the female body works. Yes, it's too early for the baby to come out. Which is exactly why I'm so worried and refused to leave, you asshole!"

"You're gonna regret callin' me an asshole later, Angel baby."

"I don't ever regret saying anything to you, buffoon."

"I thought I heard Angel keeping you in line," Reed jokes, coming up to me and tapping me on the back.

"She always is. How's your girl doin'?"

I can tell from the look on his face that Reed is scared shitless, but he's trying to keep it together. "She's doing the best that she can. Was having contractions and almost went into pre-term labor from my understanding, but I'm not a doc. All this shit is foreign to me. The gist of it is that Elena and River are gonna be okay. They gave her some special medicine that stops the contractions, but she's considered high risk now and… I think it's best that Elena stays here where the doctors can supervise her. Of course, she's giving me hell for telling her that."

"Of course. She's a spitfire."

"Yeah, but this spitfire needs to slow her ass down and keep our kid in her belly for a bit longer. I'm gonna make sure she stays here, where they can both be supervised. Only the best for my girls. Only the fuckin' best."

I nod, "They're both gonna be alright. You'll see."

"I sure hope you're right, Trick. I don't know what I'd do without them. Fuck, I haven't even met the little one yet and I already love her so much." I think for a moment that maybe I should distract him with what I just walked into, but I decide against it. I'll keep it to myself for now. Reed surely has enough to be worrying about.

CHAPTER SEVENTEEN

Ideas and plans are nice, but action is how shit gets done
~ @What Would Harvey Do

Angel

"I'm thinking we do some basic female on female shit." I hear Kyle tell Enzo, making no mistake that they're talking about the porn business for the club. From what I know, these two have really let the ball slide when it comes to their so called business. I know they were both recovering from some accidents, but at the end of the day you still need to get work done.

"Okay. How're we gonna do it?" Enzo asks him.

I'm standing in the kitchen, cooking up a storm while these two idiots are eating whatever scraps I throw them like the stray dogs they are.

Kyle chuckles loudly. I know it well. It's the type of

laugh where you think the person thinks they're the shit. "Picture this. We have two girls having a movie night. During a very intimate scene, one of them accidently touches the others boob, and BOOM that's when shit turns. She watches her and oh fuck, it's hot. It'll sell so well!"

I throw the spatula onto the counter and turn my body around to face these two buffoons. "What in the world are you two smoking?"

"Wait. Why'd you stop cooking?" Enzo asks, eyes darting from the food to what I can assume is the spatula on the counter.

I cross my arms, staring daggers into both of them. "Do you know how cliché your idea is? No woman is going to thoroughly enjoy watching that type of porn."

Kyle and Enzo look at each other, eyebrows furrowing together. "Woman?" They say at the exact same time.

"Believe it or not, women watch porn too, especially girl on girl. You two have an idea that's been repeated so many times, but from what I've heard it sounds like you both want to rush it and make it a quick video for the men's spank bank."

Enzo rises from his seat, walking to the stove to take over where I'd left off on the stir fry. Ever since the first time, I've been cooking more variations for the guys to eat. It's high in protein, has a good bit of veggies and is delicious. "You both need to remember that men and women watch porn. Personally, I love the girl on girl shit... but it has to be done in the right way to keep my attention. Are you interested in hearing my idea?"

I take their silence as a yes and continue. "Why don't you have two women in a home like setting. One is adamant that she's bi-sexual, while the other is opening her eyes up to having a sexual relationship with a woman. They drink a few glasses of wine and get a little flirty with one another. After a few kisses and tiny touches, one of the girls asks her friend to come over. Who, by the way, is a complete alpha woman. She brings her special box, which is filled with a strap-on and plenty of fun toys. The alpha chick ends up playing with both girls, makes them lick each other until they squirt and fucks them both until they can't move anymore."

I finish speaking and both look at me like I'm either batshit crazy, or the smartest bitch they've ever met. "Holy fuck. How long have you been keeping that locked up in your mind?" Kyle laughs,

I shrug lightly, "I just came up with that in the last minute and a half." Honestly, it isn't that hard for me to think about this kinda stuff.

"You wanna help us with creative... aspects of the studio? Like... a creative director?" Enzo asks me and I think about it for a minute before I nod. This could be a really good thing for me. I'll cook for the club, and then I'll just help out at the studio too. It'll be the best of both worlds, and just another way to keep me busy. Well, another way to keep my mind off of wanting a hit.

"Yeah, I can help out."

Chaos walks into the kitchen, heading straight for the cupboard and pulls his usual box of cereal out. Ever since I've been cooking, he's refused to eat anything in the fridge. "What're you *helping* with?" It's obvious by his tone that he doesn't think I'm helping at all. I really don't understand why Chaos has such a problem with me, and why he won't just give me the benefit of the doubt. I might have made mistakes in the past, but that doesn't mean I'll continue to do so. While I'll admit I'm not perfect... I would... gosh, I can't even think about where my mind is going here.

"Angel is going to help us with some ideas for the videos at the studio." Enzo tells him, wearing a sly smirk.

Chaos raises his eyebrows, "You mean she's going to be *in* the videos?"

What the fuck?! Did he say that? Chaos has said a lot of things to me, but never something like this.

"I don't know what you think I am, but I'm not a fucking slut!" I scream at him, starting to charge my body towards him.

Enzo grabs me by the elbow and shakes his head. "It's not worth it, Angel. Don't let him get to you."

I rip my arm free of Enzo's grasp and head straight for my brother, needing to say something that I've needed to for a long time. "I've done a lot of shit that I regret, and you know that. But what I have never been is a slut, and for you to keep making jabs at me like I am hurts. I haven't been the best sister and I'm sorry for that. I'm only human. I'm not some robotic thing that can be programmed in the way that you deem fit. If I was, you might even love me. But, I'm not. Instead, I'm just your little failure of a drug addict sister. I'm sorry that I'm so fucking disappointing to you, Chaos." I snarl it out, trying to stay as sincere as I can before I charge back to Trick and I's room. There's only one place I want to be right now, hiding under our comforter, trying not to think about how much my older brother hates me.

CHAPTER EIGHTEEN

Don't trust everything you see. Even salt looks like sugar
~ YourTango

Trick

Reed sent out a group text to all of the brothers about twenty minutes ago, telling us all that we needed to haul ass back to the club for an emergency session of church. In all the years that I've known him, there's only been a handful of time that he's called a session on so short notice. It just tells me that whatever we're about to find out is a big fuckin' deal.

We're all in the room, most of us standing because he told everyone that we had to be here. Even some older Nomads who don't normally come around these parts are sitting in on this. With every moment that I'm here, I just know a bomb is about to be dropped. There's no way this is gonna be something light and fluffy. The door comes blazing open and it shuts just as quickly as it opened. Reed keeps his hand on the closed door for a moment before he directs his attention at the group of us. "I was just made aware of some very… concerning news,"

This is the first time he's been away from Elena since he's made her ass stay in the hospital. Even if she wanted to come home, she can't. I don't really know the details of what's wrong with her, but I don't need to. "I'm sure you all remember Trick went away for a while because of me. He took the fall for a crime I committed, and showed us that he's a true brother, willing to make any sacrifice for the better of the club. Trick lost much more than any of us did, though. His sister, Janine and her two boys were murdered as retaliation. A few of you in this room should remember that day. How we couldn't fathom what was happening. How we needed to find out who was behind it. Today, I put all of the pieces together." Reed's stare is focused on me. "I'm so sorry, Trick. I should have seen this years ago, before anything else happened."

I take in a deep breath, never thinking that this day would come. Fuck! "Well, spit it out." I urge him, needing to know whatever information he knows.

"We had a snake in our club…for a very long time. One who we just recently discovered is nothing but a traitorous, vile snake."

Kyle shoots up from his seat, spitting out a name we

all recognize. "Max," His voice is more of a territorial growl than anything. I know Max has crossed a few people as of late, Kyle and Michelle being two of them, but that was before I came back.

Reed doesn't nod, or even so much as confirm Kyle's assumption. By the stressed look Reed's wearing, I know Kyle's right. "Max isn't just a traitor. He was a planted spy who never gave up on his mission to rip our club apart, even when his commander died all those years ago. Trick, I killed his brother. Max killed your sister and nephews as retaliation for something I did, and I cannot apologize enough for that. I want to make it up to you, but I know that nothing I do will ever make up for it."

I want to say something. Somehow deep inside me, I know that I do. I just don't know how to feel right now. Should I be relieved that there is a name finally associated with what happened to my family? Or should I be angry at Reed for allowing such a monster into our club, a monster who pretended for years to be friends with all of us. Max visited me in prison for fuck's sake!

"What the actual fuck..." Enzo blurts out into the silent room. I couldn't have said it better myself.

"So, what was the deal? His brother told him to come here all those years ago, and then you axed him and Max didn't know what to fuckin' do after that shit so he just stayed here and pretended to be our friend when he was really blowing shit up?" Seamus hisses out, nostrils flaring in a bout of rage.

I stay quiet, wanting to see everyone else's reactions

105

to this bullshit. "He fucking framed me! He raped Michelle… he killed Trick's family…what the fuck else did he do!?" Kyle roars out into the room, slamming both of his fists down onto the table.

"Who knows. At this point, I don't think I know anything anymore. Everything I thought I knew has gone down the drain." Reed says to the group of us.

"I see a lot of shit coming, but I never saw any of this." Enzo says, shaking his head in a state of disbelief. "I knew he was fucked up…but this."

"I wish I could say I was surprised. Hated him since the moment I met him." Dmitri speaks up.

Suddenly, everyone is speaking at once. Everyone's voices mesh together in a dysfunctional mess, talking so loud that I can't even think. "Shut up!" I scream, bringing the room to a complete standstill, no one daring to use their vocal cords. I stare at Reed, trying to hold my anger back. "What's your plan, Prez? Cause you've got one, don't you? We're not letting him get away with this. I want blood, Reed and by God, I'm going to get it."

Retribution has long awaited me, and I refuse to wait another minute longer.

Max has caused us all a great deal of harm, and I think it's past time that he pays for everything he's done to us.

CHAPTER NINETEEN

Growth is painful. Change is painful. But nothing is as painful as staying stuck somewhere you don't belong.
~ @BestSayings

Angel

"Holy crap! Oh my fudge-sticks!" I whip my head around to see Daisy jumping up and down for joy. She's a little bit off the wall to begin with, but never have I seen her like this. She mostly keeps to herself.

I rub the pot that I'm cleaning in and out with a sponge, watching Daisy stare at her phone sporting the biggest grin I've ever seen from her. "Everything okay over there?"

She eagerly nods, "Hell yeah! Elena just had the baby." At that, shock takes over my entire body. I'm not a doctor or anything, but I know she isn't at full term.

My heart races in my chest as I ask the question that I need an answer to. "What? Are they okay?"

"Elena is fine. River is in the NICU," She mutters it out as she leaves the kitchen. All I want to do is press her for more answers, but the reality is that all I can do right now is wonder if the baby is okay. For some reason, the fight with Jenna keeps coming to my mind. I just feel like if we had never gotten into that stupid fight, Elena wouldn't have been in the hospital in the first place. She wasn't stressed or anything before that happened, and...oh God.

If anything happens to that baby, it's only going to be one person's fault.

Mine.

I finish scrubbing the pot, probably cleaning it extra well as my mind overtook me, and wash it under cold water before I set it on the drying rack. "Look at you hard at work," Trick says upon his arrival in the kitchen.

I give him a soft smile, "Even though I'm helping out in the studio, I still need to do the cooking around here. Otherwise, y'all will just end up eating those nasty little chocolate cakes again."

"I happen to like those nasty chocolate cakes," He teases. I don't know why he does. They're disgusting, and even worse for you.

He crosses his arms, leaning his body against the island in the center of the kitchen and surveys me. "What's up with you? Something's wrong."

"Nothing is wrong," I tell him, trying my hardest to convince myself of what I've just said to him.

"Yeah, that's bullshit if I've ever heard it."

I let out a deep breath, tossing my hands up in the air. "You always think that something is wrong with me. Have you ever considered that something isn't wrong and maybe I'm just thinking... or something? Nothing has to be wrong, Trick!"

"Okay, now I know you're hiding some shit 'cause you never get this testy with me unless you are. What's buggin' you?"

I yell at him in response, *"Nothing!"* He cocks his head back and takes a good look at me. Dammit, I know I've proven his point. Fuck! "Okay. Maybe I'm thinking that if anything happened to the baby it would be my fault."

"Why in the hell would you think something like that?" The way he asks it is like he doesn't remember how Elena got into the hospital in the first place. She's there because of *me*.

I sigh, crossing my own arms, hoping that they'll offer me some sort of comfort. "Elena went into the hospital after that fight, and if anything happens, it's going to be my fault."

Trick cackles, and I know that laugh. It's the one he lets out when he's annoyed or can't believe something. "Do you realize how crazy you sound? Elena going into pre-mature labor is in no way, shape, or form your fault. You can't control all that woman mumbo-jumbo down *there*." He points to my vagina as he says it and while I want to laugh, I can't.

"You just don't get it," I mumble, walking past him into the hallway. I head towards our room, not wanting to be near Chaos right now, who is no doubt in the club playing pull. He's just going to make me feel even worse than I already do.

Just as I'm opening the door to our bedroom, I'm being grabbed by the back of the wrist and twirled around. My back is slammed against the doorframe and Trick is staring me down like I've lost my damn mind. When in fact, I think it's the exact opposite. What the hell has gotten into him? "I get everything you tell me. Every single thing I understand. There's not anything you will ever say to me that I don't understand, even if I'm actin' like it doesn't make a lick of sense to me. You shouldn't be worryin' about shit you can't control, Angel. It's not gonna do you any good and will just eat away at you and make you feel worse about yourself. Trust me, I've been there so many times and I'm still tryin' to figure out how to deal with it."

His words confuse me. Trick is many things, but never would I take him for the type of man who is critical on himself. If he is, he's hiding it so well. "What do you mean?" I ask, allowing my curiosity to get the best of me. Trick and I are still getting to know one another, and I'm betting that we'll be doing this for a pretty long fucking time. It's only been a few weeks, but we've already learned so much about the other. Truthfully, I want to keep learning more. I want to know him on the inside as well as I know his body on the outside.

I run my fingers along his face, his thick unshaved hairs scratching against my skin. "You can tell me anything, Trick." I can see the dilemma flashing across his face, fighting the urge to want to keep whatever this secret is from me.

"You and I have a habit of beating ourselves up more than necessary. You're doin' it about Elena and the baby, and I torture myself thinkin' about my sister and nephews."

Sister and nephews? I didn't even know he had any family. This doesn't make an ounce of sense. "I don't understand."

"My family died because of me. I'm responsible for their deaths and the weight of that is heavy on my shoulders every day. Not to mention, it's a constant headfuck."

"Oh my god... Trick, I'm so sorry." Emotion floods through me. I hurt for him. I hurt because he's hurting every single day and I can't even imagine how it's destroying him bit by bit. I just want to take every ounce of his pain and give it to me, for him to never feel it again.

I've always wondered why he's appeared to be so reclusive, and now I finally understand why.

CHAPTER TWENTY

Instead of trying to control every aspect of your life, give your
life the chance to surprise you from time to time.
~ Anonymous

Trick

I wake up out of a dead sleep, feeling the shift of weight on me. For some reason the past couple of nights I've been getting shit sleep. Lately, if there's so much as a clicking clock hand that's moving out of synchrony, I'm awake. I've been like this ever since I was a kid. Angel and I had a long day of chatting, and even went out into town for a steak. For once, it was nice to get away from the club and do something for ourselves.

The feel of her soft hand palming my cock jolts me into the moment. I look over to take a quick glance at my bedside clock, and it reads just past one in the morning. I'm startin' to think now I should start calling Angel my midnight minx. "Someone's in a mood," I growl at her, barely seeing her silhouette in the darkness of our room. If I squint my eyes closed enough, I can see the outline of her body.

She lets out a soft giggle, "You've been neglecting me lately," Angel wants to tease me right now, and lord I will let her.

I could be a dick and remind her of how busy we've both been. It's not easy being part of this club. There's always a load of shit to be doing. But I don't say any of it, instead I shut my fuckin' mouth and let the girl keep her tight grip on my cock. She leans down and I feel a bit of wetness spilling over me. She keeps the same grasp on me, her movements growing stronger and faster.

"You're so sweet...I *might* just lick you up and down."

This is only the second time we've had sex, and I say *had* because that's straight where this shit is leading. The first time, I might've scared her a good bit. Using my cock as a weapon to destroy her inside and out. Now, she's turning all sexual goddess on me.

Don't think I mind, cause I sure as hell don't. "You're going to lick my cock clean after I cum in that pretty little cunt of yours, but first, you'll ride." I inform her, my dominant side coming out full force.

Since the beginning I've had training wheels on my relationship with Angel, because quite frankly we needed them. After knowing her these few weeks, even with them flying by and not knowing her for an extended period of time, I know her. Or at least, I know part of her. She's not the sensitive girl everyone thinks that she is. She's much stronger than that, even if she doesn't fully believe it.

The feel of her pussy sliding over my cock is enough to pull me back in the moment. Her wet walls encase me, offering a syphoning grip. I've been with a lot of women, and I can say that none of them have ever taken me the way Angel does. She doesn't bitch or complain. She trusts that her body will adjust to me, and it does.

"Jesus!" She moans, flipping her hair in my face. I place my arm behind her head and pull her hair closer to me, clutching her locks between my fingers.

I yank her down to me, hissing out my words. "The only name you call when you're riding my cock is mine."

A sinister giggle is all I get in return as she rotates her hips on me, doing something I've never felt before. Fuck! This girl knows how to use her body. I swear, she's a seductive witch. Her lips graze over mine lightly in a teasing manner, but just as she pulls away I tug her back in my direction, biting her bottom lip with ferociousness.

I smile as I do it, feeling the way her pussy tightens even further around me. My little Angel loves a bit of pain. I'll make a note of that. Quickly, I rock myself in and out of her, both of our movements matching the other. Letting go of her lip, I slide my hand down between her legs and rub that pearled over clit of hers.

"Such a sensitive girl," I tell her, feeling her legs shake over mine.

I know she's cumming sooner rather than later, so I rub her pearl as quickly as I can, needing to feel herself spill over me. "Tr-ick...Trick!" She screams out, her nails dig into my shoulders as she stops moving her body. I continue slamming myself into her, pulling out and trying to fit my entire cock inside her. I know it'll never happen. I'm far too big for her tiny cunt.

Liquid flows over my cock as she cums around me. "That's my girl!" I continue to tease her clit, keeping her body reacting the way I want it to. She ebbs and flows, gouging her nails further into my skin. Fuck, I hope she leaves marks. Her breathing increases, sounding like she's run five miles in just a couple of minutes. She pulls herself off of me, moves to the end of the futon and positions her mouth over my cock, twirling her tongue around the side.

"No," I say to her, rising up from the couch.

I can't see her face, but I'm betting she's lookin' pretty pissed that I told her no. She just has to wait. I have something planned. "Lay on your back, head falling off the end of the futon." She does as I tell her, flipping her body around so that her legs are in the air and her head hangs off the bottom of the futon.

I line my cock up with her mouth, and tap her cheek, telling her to open. "Hum, cause I'm not gonna be easy on you, girl."

The feel of her tongue greets the head of my cock and

I want to control myself just a little bit. Especially since this is the first time, but my God...she is too tempting. I can't hold back. I can't even try to hold back. Slamming my cock inside her mouth, my cock reaches the back of her throat and I feel her gag reflex kicking in. "Hum!" I order her, feeling the vibrations of her voice around me.

In and out I move quickly, my cock growing harder with every thrust. My head swells, forming into a hard mushroom as I feel the heat rising. I want to fuck her mouth longer, but fuck! I can't. "Fuck, Angel!" I hiss out at her, grabbing her by the neck as my seed spills down her throat. "Fuck, take it all."

I pull myself out of her mouth slowly, rubbing the head of my cock over her face before I dip down and kiss her, tasting both of us on her lips.

There is nothing that compares to this – not one damn thing.

I wake up from the best night of my fuckin' life. All Angel and I did was fuck the living hell out of one another, all night long. We stopped a few times for tiny little naps, but holy shit. I wanna say I could do that shit every night, but she exhausts the living hell out of me.

Sliding on a pair of jeans, I quietly head out of our room to sneak a cigarette break. Heading towards the front door, Reed calls me over. "You have a minute?"

I stop in my tracks and shrug, "Sure. What's up?"

"We need to talk privately." He says, rising from the couch. I follow him back into the room that we've dubbed his office, when the reality of it is that the only thing he's doing in here is fuckin' Elena blind. We've all heard it. As I shut the door, he begins to speak. "It's not a surprise that Max needs to be dealt with, and since River is here... she is my concern. Keeping her and her mother safe is my only concern. You know as well as I that isn't possible if he's still walking this earth."

I've never done this, but I don't care about disrespecting him right now. "Let me."

Reed crosses his arms, lips in a stern line, telling me that he's not happy. "If you'd let me finish, then you'd know I'm asking you to do that. Max has been spotted back in New York City, and since we now know that Rage is alive... we know where he's going. He's heading to the Iron Vex MC. Rumor has it that the old Demons of Hell members who didn't get slaughtered, ran straight to Boss. They knew she'd patch them in since her ol'man is Rage. Of all the places in this world, the only place Max is safe is with a man as insane as him. There's only one person who is, and he's with his daughter, comin' back from the dead and shit. I need you to grab three of the brothers and head to New York as soon as possible. You can't take Slash with you, though."

"Jesus. You really think I don't know jack shit."

Reed's eyes widen. "What the fuck?"

"I know Slash isn't welcome around those parts. Prison confined me, it didn't keep me from hearin' all the gossip and club shit. I might've missed a little bit, but I didn't miss everything. Give me more credit than that, Reed. Shit."

"Just get going. We don't have any time to waste." I could stand here and fuck around with him for a few more minutes, but at the end of the day I know he's right. Max needs to be dealt with, and it needs to be sooner rather than later.

CHAPTER TWENTY-ONE

Direction is so much more important than speed. Some are going nowhere, fast
~ Anonymous

Trick

"I don't understand. What do you mean you have to go out of town for a few days?" Angel questions. This is the first time I've had to leave her, and I'm not gonna lie... it's making me so fucking nervous that it's not even funny. I'm worried about everything. I'm worried someone won't be around and she'll get down in one of her moods and decide to go get high. It's why I was calculating when deciding who the fuck I'm bringing with me on this trip.

The only thing Chaos ever does is upset his sister, so it's a given that I'm bringing him with me. Dmitri hates

Max more than anyone, even more than Kyle if that's possible. Lastly, I'm bringing Seamus… cause' he's built like a tank and we're likely to have people think twice about fucking with our group if he and I are standin' side by side.

"Why you… though. That's what I don't understand. Why can't it be someone else?"

I place my hands on her shoulders and stare directly into her soft eyes. "Baby, Reed asked me to go which means I have to. We've known each other for a long time and he trusts me. Plus, this is personal for me."

She squints her nose together, trying to piece together the puzzle. She's not going to, though. Angel doesn't know about certain parts of my past. "I don't…"

Before she even finishes, I cut her off. "Max killed my sister and nephews." Her eyes grow wide within nanoseconds, but I continue. "He's hurt a lot of us here. Some more than others. I want to take him down, Angel, and I have to do it. The fact that he's still breathing while my sister and those kids are six feet under kills me. It fuckin' kills me…"

"Those are the names you say at night…" She whispers, saying it so quietly that I barely hear her.

"Huh?"

"Usually a few times every night you thrash around and get sweaty in your sleep. You always say Cody and Josh." Dammit. I had no idea I do this shit in my sleep.

I nod once at her, "Yeah. That would be them."

She pushes her lips over to the right, obviously not

likin' that I'm leavin. "You have to do what you have to do. But… Trick?"

"Yeah?"

"Make sure he suffers. Whenever you get him, make sure that he's paying for everything he's done."

It's music to my ears hearin' her say that. I move my hands from her shoulders to encase her face, givin' her one of those kisses that the girls love to talk about in the chick flicks.

"Romeo, we've got some shit to discuss!" I hear Kyle's voice booming at me, and he doesn't sound the least bit pleased. "Romeo!" He repeats, sounding even more irritated than the first time.

I glare at him as I speak, "What?!"

"You're going to New York after this motherfucker and you didn't think of asking me to go with you?"

"Reed told me to bring three, not the entire club."

"And you're taking Chaos?" Kyle chastises.

I look over to Angel, "That is why I'm bringing Chaos. He's always a dick to her anyway. No way in hell I'd leave him here to torment her."

"Whoa. You're babysitting my brother so he won't be a dickbag to me?" Angel asks like it's shocked her.

I bring my brows together, "Yeah. Why wouldn't I?"

She gives me a lighthearted smile. "Wow. You must really love me."

I start to say something to Kyle when I catch what Angel just said. She didn't say care. She said *love*. "I do, very much." My reply comes out of me so naturally, and

I'm glad it does 'cause I need her to know how I feel about her. She's the most precious thing in my entire life. My one chance at happiness and having the family I've always wanted for myself.

I see my reply finally registers with her. Maybe she didn't even realize what she said at first, and knowing her, it just slipped out. She is one of the most heartfelt women I've ever known, but with that comes a guarded part of herself that she doesn't allow anyone to get past. Somehow, some way... I've managed to break past her walls, and I couldn't be happier. I only hope she is too.

"Point and case being I'm coming with you all and there's nothing you can do to stop my stubborn ass." Kyle grumbles out, getting the last word in. I shake my head, not even bothering to argue with him. "Alright, but you're the one with a pregnant girlfriend."

"Michelle will be fine. She's a tough bitch." He says to me as he walks away. Sometimes I wonder how a man like Kyle, er, let me rephrase that. I wonder how a *dick* like Kyle landed a girl like Michelle.

I kiss Angel quickly on the lips, "Babe. I have to get my shit together. I love you, and I'll see you in a few days."

CHAPTER TWENTY-TWO

We are what we repeatedly do. Excellence, then, is not an act,
but a habit
~ Aristotle

Angel

It feels so fucking weird to be here by myself. It's not like I'm alone or anything, but it *feels* like I'm alone when Trick isn't around. I hate to be that girl who says that part of her is missing when their boyfriend isn't around, but I'm totally pulling that card.

I feel like there is a huge part of me missing, and because of that, I almost feel sick. I don't feel happy, but I don't feel sad either. I just feel... void, here, like a waste of space. "What's up with you looking all sad and shit?" Enzo asks from the beanbag chair in the corner of the studio.

I know what the actors did on that chair yesterday and I sure wouldn't be sitting there...

Yuck!

I swivel around on the computer chair to face him, bringing my legs up to where I'm sitting pretzel style. "I'm fine. I just miss him. I'm worried... I think."

"Has he been texting you?"

I nod.

"Has he called you?"

I nod.

"Then why the hell are you worried? He's alive and well. If he wasn't, you wouldn't be hearing from his ass."

I huff, "I don't know. I'm not used to this yet, Enzo. Every bit of this is so new to me and I don't know how I'm supposed to handle it."

"Want me to tell you a secret?" Why do I feel like this isn't much of a secret, and more of him being a smartass? "You just have to keep busy and deal with it. There's nothing else you can do, and it sucks. But if you don't just keep yourself busy, you're gonna think about it all the time and that is gonna drive you crazy. Your head will muster up the worst things that could be happening and you'll be over here freaking out while he's eating a slice of deep dish pizza. We just need to distract your wandering mind."

"Okay, wise one. Distract me."

"Ask me something. Believe it or not, you don't know that much about me."

"What's your full name?"

"Lorenzo Giuseppe Bianchi," I thought he was gonna shoot out something short, but lord I didn't expect that. His last name rings a bell, though. "I can tell by the face you're making that you've heard of the Bianchis."

I think hard and I know that I have, I just don't know how. Wait a second. "Aren't they some old fashioned gangsters?"

He nods. "Yep. Straight outta New York. My father's family runs the streets up there."

"Whoa. WHOA. So… you're like… Italian royalty."

Enzo chuckles, "No, not quite. I'm not a DiGiovanni. My dad is a low-life scumbag, and he was an even worse father."

"Oh… sorry."

"There's nothing to apologize for. See what this is doing? You're keeping your mind off of Trick. Ask me another question."

Oh, this one will be easy. "How in the hell are you still single?"

Now for this question Enzo doesn't respond as quickly, "I'm hung up on a girl that I don't even think knows I exist. I've wanted her for ages, but on top of that, her brother loathes me and she loves her brother."

"Aw. That's sad." I tell him, meaning every word of it. I can't imagine wanting someone so badly, but feeling like it would never work out because of their family. So much so, that you don't even give it a shot. "Don't let the fear of what might happen hold you back from what can." I don't know where the words of wisdom just came from. But if I've learned anything in life, it's that you have to chase after what you want, even if it terrifies you half to death.

CHAPTER TWENTY-THREE

Don't give up on something you really want
~ Anonymous

Trick

Queens is one of the places where I'd rather not be. Honestly, I have no desire to ever be slammed in the midst of congestion central. Out of everything in this world, I hate traffic the most. Another prison sentence would be easier on me than this shit is. I raise my hand up, seeing that we're just a block away from the Iron Vex clubhouse.

The last time I saw Boss she was a young girl, maybe nineteen or in her early twenties. It's been a few years. I remember as a teenager, she never really cared for her father much. They have a typical deadbeat dad situation going on. Rage fucked her Mom all those years ago, she got pregnant and he showed up a few times every now and again. Which is why it makes this situation so interesting. Rage crawled back to his baby girl's front doorstep for help, bringing his leftover men with him along the way.

After ten minutes we're finally able to gain traction and get to where we need to be. The Iron Vex's club looks nothing like the rest. Being that they're in the middle of a major city, their clubhouse is a seven bay garage that goes up two stories. It's been years since I've been here, but somehow I doubt that it's changed much. I raise my hand and motion the brothers to follow me, parking our bikes on the side.

There's no chance that we'll be able to get in undetected, so I make sure that we're all in view. Each of us park our bikes, dismount and meet up. "We'll get into the bar and have a couple drinks. At some point Boss will come up and ask us what's going on no doubt." I say, not sticking around to hear their replies or disagreements with my plan. They shouldn't even have any. I've been doing this for a fuck of a long time and if I didn't know what I was doing, I wouldn't still be alive.

It might be the end of winter, but brothers still stand outside with the garage bay doors wide open, staring at us as we walk down to where the bar is. They've sectioned out an entire part of their club for this joint. No civilians can come in unless they're sponsored by a patched member. The Iron Vex have some interesting... traditions that go on certain nights of the week. Shit, who knows. They might be swingin' around every night these days.

I pull open the door to the bar and the brothers follow closely behind, each splitting away from me. We've been in this rodeo a few times, knowing it's better to break apart than to all be together. "Hey handsome. You new?" A short black girl greets me, with dreads that fall down to her ass.

"I'm old, ancient even." I reply, getting a good laugh out of her. "Say, is Boss around? I'm an old friend."

"Hmm, old I'll agree with. Friend... you don't look like a friend Boss would have. You know what I'm sayin'" She mutters before disappearing behind the bar, into what I can imagine is either the way to the stock room or kitchen. This girl seems to know a lot about Boss, and her tastes.

I hear the click of her heels hitting the wood before she even comes into view. Turning, she sways down the stairs like she always does, looking just like a goddess. The brothers look to me and then to her, none of them meeting her before. "Have you come here for your games, Trick?"

"No, ma'am. Purely business."

Boss crosses her arms, putting all of her weight on one foot, looking like the sassy bitch she is. "You have never been here for purely business. Whenever you come here... you like to stay long enough to *come... in... here.*" Before I got locked up, I would drive up to New York every few months to take part in some of the swinging

parties the Iron Vexs put on. Only thing is, I wasn't doin'
much swingin' since I was fuckin' their Prez.

I shake my head, putting my hand up. "No, love. I
have an ol'lady now and we're good. I'm here for business. There's been a guy named Max sniffin' around here
since your Pops came back?"

Her eyes go wide, telling me that no one has
confronted her about her father being alive. "I don't
know what you're talking about."

"Sure you do. Your uncle was mistakenly killed and
your Pops crawled back to you to save his sorry ass from
actually being murdered." Her eyes don't waver from
mine and I know what she's doing. Boss is trying to
figure out what her next play is. The thing is… she
doesn't have any. "I don't give a fuck about your Pops. I
just want Max."

"Why should I give you him?" She counters, trying to
play hard to get. She forgets that I know her, and I know
deep, dark secrets about her. Like the way she thinks,
and the fucked up dream that she's always wanted her
daddy in her life. Why else would she be fuckin' the older
men like myself? Daddy issues much?

"Because you don't have a choice. No one knows Rage
is alive accept for me, and just because of our history, I'll
keep that secret. If you give me Max. He's fucked us over,
girl. Murdered innocents, raped one of the Skulls girls.
That's only the shit I know about." I say. I don't want to
give her too much, but I will if I have to. If anything, this

130

girl has a heart. She'll give me what I want. "He killed Janine and the boys."

Her mouth forms into a small 'o', "Fuck."

"Yep."

"I'll give you Max, but you keep my Father out of your shit."

"I don't care about Rage. I just fuckin' want Max."

"Fine. I'm shocked you're the one up here and not Reed, though. What's up with that?"

"His wife just had a baby, so he's kinda pre-occupied. Plus, leavin' her alone right now with Max in the wind isn't exactly a smart thing to be doin'."

She nods once, understanding where I'm coming from. "Give me a second and I'll tell you where he's supposed to be going. I have him running errands for me over the next few days."

Thank fuck.

Max, you're about to get *tricked*.

CHAPTER TWENTY-FOUR

I'm not going anywhere. The only time I'll let go of your hand
is to grab your ass
~ J.M. Storm

Angel

Enzo and I went to the store to grab more groceries for
the club early this morning, but they didn't have the type
of milk I wanted so I ended up dragging his ass to three
different stores before I found it. He may not realize it,
but he likes it the best too. It's the only milk I can get the
brothers to drink. At first, I didn't think that I'd be taking
my job as kitchen cook too seriously, especially since I'm
working at the studio now too… but I do. It's important
to me that everyone is getting some nutrients in. Plus, it
distracts me and as Enzo kindly reminds me, I need
more of that.

Upon arriving back at the club I see Trick's bike parked out front and butterflies swarm over my stomach. He's been gone for eight entire days. So long that I thought he might never come back. His trip was only supposed to be three or four, and it kept getting extended. Why that is, I'm unsure.

I park the car, grab two handfuls of groceries and charge in through the front door. Not giving a care in the world that I left Enzo with an entire back seat full of stuff to carry in. He's strong. He can handle that shit.

"Trick!" I call out, looking for my man. I don't see him anywhere in sight, so I run into the kitchen and drop off the groceries then head straight for our bedroom. Maybe he's in our room! Opening the door, I glance around and see that he's not. God, this is frustrating.

I go back out into the main area of the club and wait, wondering where else it is that he could be. Church would be the only other option, but that can't be right because Enzo was with me and then I see Chaos sitting down. If church is happening… my brother would be in there too. "Hey there, porn star."

I ignore Chaos, knowing that's all I can do these days. Otherwise, whatever it is he says eats at me too much. I'm not paying a lick of attention, but the sound of skin hitting skin is enough to pull my attention that way. Maria is standing up, glaring down at him, cursing a whole bunch of words at him in Spanish. Well, I'm assuming that she's cursing because I don't speak Spanish and I have no idea what she's saying. "What the fuck is wrong with you?!" She screams at him. "Why do you always speak to her like this? It's not okay."

He scoffs, not caring because let's be real, he never does. "More like what the fuck is wrong with you, *taquita*. You don't get to judge me when you're keeping that… *thing…*" He glares at her, and I mean… this glare is something that I've never seen before. He looks at her like he hates her entire existence, worse than what he's ever done to me.

My eyes dart around the room and I try to see if anyone has heard him, but no one else is here. "I come back from being gone for days, expecting you to tell me you handled it… and it's the exact opposite. You're keeping that… devil spawn." He spits out, walking out of the main area and out towards their room.

"Maria," I say soothingly.

She puts her hand up, "No. It's okay. I expected this from him. I'm fine…" Before I can stop her, she's out the front door and I hope she's heading to Pain. He'll know exactly what to say to her.

I take in a deep breath and wonder if I should continue my search for Trick, but I know better. Instead, I head for where Chaos just disappeared to. Walking down the hallway until I reach their room, I don't bother to knock as I walk in.

He's staring out the window, completely still. Unphased by the fact his door just opened and closed.

"It's okay to be angry." My words come out of nowhere, like something is taking over my body as I speak. I don't want to be here, comforting him. The sad reality is that I know he needs it. And I know that if I don't do this right here, right now… his anger will end up destroying everything he holds dear, and then himself. "It's okay to be angry at yourself for what happened, but blaming yourself… you can't do that."

He turns himself towards me, "I didn't ask you for your opinion."

"I wasn't asking for permission, fuckface." I snap, continuing. "You love her. I know that you do, and you know you do, *and* everyone else knows you do. She told me and you have to know this is so hard for her. Do you realize how scared she is?"

Chaos doesn't say a damned thing. I want to curse and scream at him, but I don't. I just continue. "It's not that baby's fault that something awful happened to her. It's not Maria's fault that this happened to her. If she's making the decision to keep this baby, then you need to support her, Chaos. I know it's hard, and I can't imagine what it must feel like for you… but if you want your relationship with her to work… you have to love that child when it's here. You can't look at it like you hate it, and you can't judge her for the hard decision that she's had to make."

He blinks a couple of times before he brings his hand over his face and lets out a deep breath. When he removes his hand, I see the redness covering him. The fact that he's barely holding it together. He's at his limit

135

and if he's not careful... he'll crumble worse than any of us ever have.

I don't know what takes over me, because lord knows he doesn't deserve what I'm about to do. It's almost like I'm afraid that I'll change my mind if I give myself a minute to think. I rush over to him, and wrap my arms around his body, pulling him into the tightest hug I can muster up.

He coughs, and I feel his chest going up and down. His nostrils are flaring, trying to hold back the emotions that he's held in for so long. "Keeping them buried in doesn't help." I whisper, rubbing his back.

"I'm sorry," He says it quietly, putting his arms around me. "I'm sorry that I'm so cruel to you. I just can't... can't go through it all again. If I hate you, I don't care if you're dead... but if I care and something happens... I'll... I just can't."

"It's okay." I say, because I understand what he's saying more than he can fathom. It's hard loving an addict, and what Chaos sometimes forget is, that he's an addict too. Out of the three of us, he's the hardest to love. I mean, think about his serious attitude problem.

There's a light rap on the door, "Come in," I say, pulling away from my brother. Fuck! I didn't think about how he was emotional.

The door comes open and behind it is my Trick. I smile all bright eyed and bushy tailed, starting to go over to him, but he stops me. "Not now, Angel. We're having an emergency meeting of church. Be there in five, Chaos."

The guys were gone days longer than they should've been and I don't know how I didn't put it together, but that must mean something is really wrong. I just hope it's not too bad.

CHAPTER TWENTY-FIVE

She was not fragile like a flower. She was fragile like
a bomb

~ Anonymous

Trick

I can honestly say that, It seems like nothing is going our
way.. We got the information from Boss and as per usual,
we lost him. I think we're all starting to feel it now. The
disappointment, frustration and anger. Lord knows I am.

I can't understand how it is so hard to locate one man
when we have an abundance of contacts all over the
world. How is he this hard to nab? *How?*

"I don't understand it." I bring my thoughts out of my
head and say it to the brothers. Watching as a few of
them nod their heads in understanding, while others just

stay quiet. "There has to be another resource that we're not using, another way to find him, to make sure that he's not one step ahead of us."

"Do you really think he knew we'd go up to New York?" Seamus asks me, and I shrug.

"It depends how well he knows Reed, and how he thinks." I say, looking to our Prez. "He knows your mentality pretty fucking well."

Enzo sits up in his chair, "So, the answer is simple. Don't leave it up to Reed on what to do next. Max is already thinking like that... thinking about the resources that we have and what we'd use. He doesn't know about my resources, because we've never had to use them."

Reed speaks up, stating his opinion. "No. It's not an option, and I won't allow it."

Enzo scoffs, "I'm not asking for permission. I'm fuckin' tired of this bullshit. It's gone on for far too long and I have connections on both sides of my family. We've never needed to use them before and for fuck's sake... Reed. *Now* is the time where we use the pull I have. If you ask me, we're out of options."

"We have plenty of options, ones that don't pertain to using your... family." Shit. If I didn't know any better, I'd say that Reed has a problem with Enzo's family. I wonder what that's about.

"That's bullshit. We don't have any options that will work. You know that as well as I do. Let me help. Jesus, let me fucking help!"

"No. They'll want something in return." Reed shuts him down immediately, not even giving him the time of day.

The room grows quiet, no one knowing what to say next, but just as Enzo opens his mouth to speak, the door comes flying open. It's Angel and everything about the expression that's sprawled across her face tells me that something's wrong.

"What's going on?" I ask, getting up from my seat to approach her.

"I... I don't know how to say th-this." She murmurs, eyes darting all around the room. She's trying to look at everyone, but no one. There's no mistaking that she's terrified out of her damn mind.

I run my hands over her shoulders, urging her on. "It's okay, just say it."

"Bubba's just blew up." Whoa. What?!

"What do you mean?" Seamus asks her.

"Bubba's... b-blew up. It's o-on fire." At that, half of the brothers are rushing out the door to get on their bikes and see what's going on. There's no mistaking what she said. There's only piecing together what happened, but we all know who's behind it.

I look over to Enzo, "I think it's about time we use your resources."

"No. I already said no." Reed snaps at me. "You don't know who his family is."

"It can't be that fuckin' bad if he's a brother in our

fuckin' club!" I roar at him, not giving a damn for whatever amount of disrespect I'm throwin' at him.

There needs to be change, and it needs to happen soon. We can't keep doing this. None of us can.

EPILOGUE

I want to move on,
But moving on means forgetting I'm not ready to let you
go yet.
~ K. Azizian

Angel

16 years later...

"I've always known that there would be a day where I wouldn't have you by my side. I just never thought it would come so quick, that our time would run out so fast." It's only been a week since Trick passed away peacefully in his sleep, going out the way any old man would. I bring my hand up to my face and wipe away the trickling tears that somehow manage to escape, rolling slowly over my cheeks. I smile down at the gravestone, "I know I said I wouldn't keep doing this, but you know I'm an emotional old hag."

I run my hand over the grass that's already starting to grow over the dirt. Somehow, I think it will soothe me, but the only thing it does is destroy me a little bit more and more. "Mom, you ready to go?" I turn my head back and stare at our boy, who looks just like you. I fucking hate you for that, for passing on the very same features to our son. I hate that I have to stare at him because he reminds me of you and reminding me of you only does one thing – it hurts.

"Just give me a couple more minutes, sweetie." I tell Brooks. His birthday is in just a few days, and I know how badly you wanted to be here. How badly you wanted to give him his bike yourself. All these years, you told his ass that he couldn't have one until he was eighteen and even then, I knew you were full of shit. You'd never keep something so precious from him.

I make no mistake as I hear Bree click her tongue against the roof of her mouth. Something you'd surely pick on her for if you were here. We both know what's coming. "Geeze. Give her a break. Dad's dead you jerk!" Sassy and mouthy, just like me.

I whirl my body around, stopping this shit before it goes any further. "Okay. Let's go."

"Home?" Brooks ask me, and I shake my head.

"No, we're going to the club."

"Yes!" Bree jumps up and down with joy. "I can't wait. I have so much to tell the trips." The *trips*, the lovely term the kids have come up with for Michelle and Kyle's three girls. They definitely are trips all right, so the name is very fitting.

Brooks rolls his eyes and heads straight for my Jeep Wrangler. I know how hard this is for me, so I can't even imagine how hard it must be for my poor kids. Especially Brooks, he's keeping all of his emotions bottled up, but he isn't fooling me. His father's death is destroying him, and I'm seeing every bit of it under the mask he has on.

After we're all hauled into the jeep, I take the short drive over to the club. Upon arrival, I see that it's packed. Now that some of the older kids have cars and bikes, the entire lot barely has any room left. I bring the jeep up to our usual spot and park, hopping out just as the kids are. "We're going home in two hours!" I call over to Bree, who waves her hand up in understanding. She's too excited to see her friends, and I can't blame her for that. In all honesty, I'm just happy that she's able to find some happiness right now.

Brooks disappears out of sight, off to god knows where. Probably the garage out back to see what Seamus and Ryder are working on these days.

I don't waste any time and head straight inside, opening the front door to see the load of new prospects the club has. Reed is sitting in his old, worn out leather chair chatting amongst the group of them while I see Elena seated at the bar with River behind it, liquor in hand. Jesus Christ, she's not old enough to be drinking yet.

I march over and start to put in my two cents, "You'd better put down the tequila, woman. Before I cut off your hand." I warn River.

She looks right at her Mom, who only laughs. "Uh… mom told me I'd have to learn how to make drinks if I'm gonna start bartending at Bubba's."

I give Elena a look that tells her she's batshit crazy. "Oh *hell* no. What crazy juice is your momma drinking these days? You can't even hand a customer an alcoholic drink with the laws they have in effect these days. You have to be twenty-one, sweetie."

River huffs, throwing her hands up in the air. "I'm so tired of my age stopping me from all of my dreams and doing the things that I want to do."

"Did I hear you right? Did you just insinuate that working at Bubba's is a life dream of yours? You'd better aim higher pumpkin, cause that shit is sad." I say, not regretting a word of it. River is the smartest girl in this joint. Her mom is an ex-FBI field agent, her father is one of the strongest MC Prezs around… and this little girl wants to work in a bar. No, it's not adding up. She slams the bottle of tequila down on the bar so hard that it breaks and runs off down the back hallway.

"You know she hates it when you're sarcastic and pushy with her," Elena chastises me.

"You two can't keep sheltering her. She's practically an adult, and she needs to experience the world for what it is these days. Brutal and awful."

Elena cocks her head in my direction, "The world

isn't as tough on all of us as it was for some of us. She needs to go through her own experiences." She takes in a deep breath and I can already tell she's going to ask what I don't want her to. Placing her hand on my belly, she rubs gently. "How are the two of you holding up, all things considered?"

"As good as a seven-month pregnant lady can after her husband randomly died in his sleep." The words come out rushed because I have to shove them out before I get myself upset. Never did I see myself here, alone... pregnant at my age with two teenagers on my hands. This baby was a surprise to say the least, but a welcome one at that.

"Did you decide on a name yet?" I'd thought long and hard about a name for my little guy. Trick and I got in so many fights over the last few weeks because we just couldn't seem to agree on a name that would be fitting. After everything that's happened, I think I've finally come up with the perfect one.

I smile, trying to hide the pain behind my words. "Yeah. TJ. Short for Trick Junior."

No matter what obstacles we may face my children and I, we'll stand strong and overcome them.

Dear Reader,

I know there's a good chance y'all may hate me for finishing the book like that. I thought about writing another ten chapters in this bad boy, but then Retribution (Skulls Renegade MC #10) wouldn't be out to y'all for another couple months and I just couldn't do that to you. Plus, it needed to end here. I hope you enjoyed Angel & Trick as much as I loved writing them. Don't worry, I sobbed like a baby bitch too when I was writing the epilogue.

In Retribution, we pick up right after the club finds out about the bombing. It will be in multiple POV, but mainly Enzo's...and his lady friend's.

I can't believe we're here, and I'm starting to write the last book in the Skulls Renegade MC series.

Thank you all for your support,

Xoxo

Liz

Made in the USA
Coppell, TX
30 December 2021

70444591R00090